ALL CREATURES OF OUR G.O.D. AND KING

by

Barbara Bayley

"All creatures of our God and King, lift up your voices, let us sing: Alleluia, alleluia!

Bright burning sun with golden beams, pale silver moon that gently gleams,

O praise him, O praise him, Alleluia, alleluia, alleluia!"

Words: St. Francis of Assisi (1182-1226); hymn number 400, 1982 Episcopal Hymnal.

"There's a wideness in God's mercy/Like the wideness of the sea."

Frederick Faber (1814-1863); hymn number 470, 1982 Episcopal Hymnal.

(with thanks to TraMi)

I. The Gambe Stop Gambit and Leland Frye flap

> "One of the current hazards of organ-building is that after you've designed and placed an organ as well as you possibly can, some well-meaning lady is able to ruin the whole thing by donating memorial carpeting to the church."
>
> Dr. Robert Baker, organist, *The New Yorker*, Dec. 23, 1961.

Perhaps the wreckage of my marriage could be traced back to the disagreement over the Gambe stop for the new church organ.

Then I would also have to blame Mrs. Gustafson.

Old Mrs. Gustafson, childless and alone after her beloved flea-infested Burmese feline died, on her own way to meet her Maker just a month later, begged me to reassure her that there was an animal kingdom in heaven and she and Cat-Mandoo would meet again.

Every chair in Mrs. Gustafson's bedroom was piled high with cat magazines and cat hair, so I stood over her bed to pray with her. When I patted her transparent hand, she pulled mine beneath her quilts so that it landed palm-flat on her aged naked belly. I pretended this had not happened. I smiled at her, pulled my hand back, touched the starched white halo of my collar as though I had an itch (it may well have been a residual flea), and told her that God was able to perform many miracles indeed!

"Father George--lean down so I can tell you something," she muttered. I saw the glint in her eye just before she kissed me, her breath rank, on the lips. I only hope my parishioners know what I go through just to keep the peace among them!

Anyway, Mrs. Gustafson changed her will *on the spot*, leaving money for an organ for my parish, St. Swithun's Episcopal Church, here in Banana Bay, Florida. And as its new rector, just a fresh three months in, I feel that I have the final say as to which stops should be incorporated into the new pipe organ.

Oh yes, it will be a pipe organ.

I have strong feelings about music and especially about the way music sounds, not just the way it is written on the printed page. I happen to believe that the Gambe sound is a pleasing one, just nasal and spicy enough—I daresay a nutmeg overtone with a dab of ginger-- to bring a congregation to its feet readily as everyone sings hymn number 671, "Amazing Grace".

Thus I spoke at our first organ committee meeting, firmly.

So I was astounded when our own Mr. Leland Frye, our new organist, all but held his nose at the mention of "Gambe".

"And *puh-lease* may we confine that particular hymn to funerals and any services we have for older people?" he had the audacity to ask me, right in front of the committee!

This same music committee had hired Mr. Frye after our venerable organist Miss Peabody's unfortunate accident. I was alone in protesting. "He is young and I am not sure he knows what the Episcopal liturgy is all about," I had stated. "He comes straight from college and the Seventh Day Adventist church."

Oh, yes. *Now* they were getting the whirlwind that they had reaped: Leland Frye, only just now learning the Episcopal seasons and colors, was arguing against the use of one of my old favorite standards.

"If you consider the history of this hymn and how it speaks against slavery—," trilled Mrs. Hitchcock, looking to me for support.

"I don't mind that," interrupted Mr. Frye calmly, rising to his well-toned height of six feet. "I mind that people *swoop* the words. It's not a dirge, you know." And he started to sing, "Ama-azing grace, ho-ow sweet the sound/Tha-at saved a wretch li-ike me," and he sang as if he were swinging in a swing, up and down, up and down.

It was an *insufferable* interruption to what should have been a cut-and-dried meeting, despite his rich tenor. What a shame, I had thought so many times this past week, to have hired an organist with such a beautiful voice, a man who is trying to direct the choir while playing our old unreliable electronic organ. He should be singing solos, except how would that have looked—Mr. Frye accompanying himself in church like some-- chanteuse in a tavern!

Leland Frye swept his right hand through his thick blond hair and I watched as in knee-jerk reaction the two men on the committee did the same thing to their thinning grey ones. Mrs. Hitchcock now wore a couple of bright spots on her fading cheeks and her eyes were big with—was that *admiration*?—as she nodded at Mr. Frye.

Surely not! Gladys Hitchcock was one of my most stalwart supporters, no matter what I suggested. Had she not gone along with my idea of letting the unruly Wee Ones Choir only sing on Mother's and Father's Days? And she had stood firm with me against the use of a praise music songbook. Call that stuff *music*! I thought now and snorted despite myself.

"We will table the choice of stops for the new organ until we can get a representative group of people to do more information gathering," said Mr. Foster rather loudly, since he refused to believe his family's arguments that he was becoming hard of hearing.

There was a scraping of chairs as all stood so that I could intone a final blessing. So. Nothing accomplished. I should have realized. Well, I was determined that I myself would be the head of that group and I would have something to say about the insertion of the Gambe stop in the new organ, come heck or high water!

*   *   *

"Father George, I have a list of stops you might be interested in. I compiled them when I was studying organ in high school and I've been revising my list ever since. I think you would be satisfied. Of course, some of them can be coupled—"

We stood outside in the mild November Florida night air. Mrs. Hitchcock was pulling on his shirtsleeve for attention and he smiled down at her. I let him talk, but I was not about to start an argument here and now. I would, after all, have the final say in the matter.

Leland's list was clean and neat. I could tell that he was more proficient than I on the computer. This for some reason upset me further, but I was not about to let him see that.

Our eyes met for a moment, he looking down, I looking up. His expression was obvious to me: "You might be able to get that Gambe stop installed on the new organ, but *I'm* the one who will decide to use it or not."

"And, Father George, I really should have mentioned this earlier, but—have you done any measurements, or had a pipe organ specialist here yet? A pipe organ will not fit into the church—there's not enough space for one."

"Nonsense."

"I've done some research, sir. You might be surprised. Now, the new electronics sound just like pipe organs, without the upkeep--."

Insufferable!

Well. *You* may be twenty-five years old, young man, I thought; but I have another almost fifteen years of experience over yours. And (my trump card always) I am a Cradle Episcopalian. And I pride myself on *never* being surprised.

*   *   *

I enclose my first sermon to the congregants of St. Swithun's, as an example of my erudite yet down-to-earth manner of presenting the Good Word. I have shortened it here, but the reader (which unfortunately shall be only myself, since this is my private journal, unless I decide to edit and publish it someday) will appreciate the flavor of my words:

"Good morning, my people who Call Ourselves Christians: I decided that instead of preaching the Good News to you, I would give you a bit of musical background, and this concerns one Ithamar Conkey—and is it not peculiar that we do not meet anyone today named Ithamar?"

(Pause for laughter.) "Ithamar Conkey was the organist" (smile and nod to Miss Peabody at the organ) "in 1849 at the Central Baptist Church in Norwich, Connecticut." (Pronounce it correctly—*Norrich*.) "One Sunday in Lent the weather was so nasty and cold that most of the parishioners did not show up for the service, unlike you, in this delightful state of Florida with such seasonal weather every day." (That is good—let them know I like their state, whether true or not.)

"Mr. Conkey had spent a great deal of time rehearsing the choir" (smile and nod to the choir) "but only one lone member dared all the dreary darkness of that day" (will they catch the alliteration? I hope so) "—a soprano, standing smiling in her sopping shawl." (More alliteration. Turn toward Mrs. Hitchcock, our soprano, and smile.)

"Mr. Conkey was so depressed and discouraged that he did something he had never done before: he shut and locked the organ and went home. No one seemed to notice. At home he could not get the words "In the cross of Christ I glory" out of his head; and as he sat at his piano a melody poured forth to those words. We sing that melody even today." (Do not tell them the hymn number yet or they will start fumbling through their hymnals.)

"He named it 'Rathbun'. And why, you ask, did he give that name to his hymn tune? Why, to honor no less than the faithful soprano who had ventured out into the miserable weather to sing: Mrs. Beriah S. Rathbun." (Look meaningfully at the congregation.) "We all need a Mrs. Rathbun in our lives, to give us cheer and encouragement when things do not appear so pleasant. Perhaps the person seated beside you will turn out to be your Mrs. Rathbun.

"Mayhap, and I say this in all humility, *I* shall in the future be your own Mrs. Rathbun, coming through any kind of weather to be of assistance, riding up on my white horse, as it were, like St. George fighting the dragon" (will they get the reference to my name and St. George?) "to shore up your faltering beliefs and woes. Perhaps *God Himself* has sent me to you for this reason. Time itself will tell. Amen."

"And now let us turn in our hymnals to hymn 441 and celebrate Ithamar Conkey's tune with our voices, joined in song. Miss Peabody, if you please." (Choir stands.)

Yes, the choir stood and sang—and what was that low droning I heard, like a bagpipe as the air leaves it? The sound reminded me of a record I had been forced to listen to as a young college student—something about jazz—ah, yes!-- Erroll Garner, the jazz musician, who would hum along, always off-pitch, to his own piano playing.

"Hear that guy? Boy, this record will someday be a collector's item," my roommate would announce to me *ad nauseum*, but all I could hear was the discord.

What *is* it? I now tried to place the sound. And there it was—unhappily, in the choir itself. I watched as the various five choir members struggled with an anthem that needed at least three more rehearsals and ten more singers to overcome. That dreadful buzzing sound was not Mrs. Hitchcock—I would know her vibrato anywhere. Not Mr. Campbell or Mr. Foster—the sound was too high for them. Could it be the quiet petite Miss Elliott?

Aha!--*there* it was, in the form of Miss Agnes Brown. A rather nasal sound, almost like an oboe, emanated from her, as though the music were being transmitted through the nose instead of the throat. I then became aware that Miss Elliott was doing her utmost to hold the alto section together, but it was rather like a rescuer being pulled beneath the waves by the one she was struggling to save.

Now this is one of my pet peeves as a clergyman: parishioners who are determined to sing in the choir. If someone knows nothing about roofing, does he insist on getting up on the top of the bell tower to nail down shingles? If someone knows absolutely nothing at all about plumbing, does he start taking apart the sink in the parish hall kitchen? If someone cannot balance his own checkbook, does he feel compelled to be the church treasurer?

So why then against all odds does someone say to him/herself, "I know nothing at all about music. I cannot carry a tune and I cannot even read notes. Therefore, *I think I shall join the choir*!"

Actually, I believe I know the answer: when David said, "Let us make a joyful noise unto the Lord," the non-musical followers actually obeyed him.

So on I struggled this first half-year in vain to get these people to need me; but they seemed content with their choir, their organist, their prayer circles, their blue church. They liked my new wife Gail, I could tell. They accepted her daughter Amber easily into the Youth Program. Oh, I worked tirelessly to become their spiritual leader, their St. George—but they just did not appear to *need me*!

Is it any wonder that I enjoyed more and more my time alone in my den with a drink or two, while I mulled over the vexing problem of how to be more needed?

II. In which George Introduces Himself

> "I should have been a pair of ragged claws
>
> Scuttling across the floors of silent seas."
>
> T.S. Eliot: The Love Song of J. Alfred Prufrock

I confess to you straight out: I do not understand why God made Florida.

Oh, I understand full well why He made New England—it was to force us to stay inside during the winter and ruminate upon our shortcomings and sins and to celebrate the coming of spring, that harbinger of Easter joys.

But *Florida!* Where the earth never hardens, where the ponds never freeze over. Where there seems to be no need or desire for introspection and repentance! An entire repository of colors, smells, sights—everything is so *overblown* here! Do you want a bird? Well, there's a flamingo or a white pelican over there. How about a daisy? No, no—you must have jasmine or a gardenia, whose scent is enough to put one into a lethean mindlessness.

Nothing somber about the garb of the citizens, either—where are the blacks and greys I am used to? No, not even at funerals! It is as if they are saying, "This is life and let us get on with it!" They are all so cheerful, even while sweating!

I am convinced that if the Mayflower had landed in Banana Bay, Florida, ours would now be a Godless country. I pray every day to be worthy enough to show my parishioners the errors of their ways. I pray that this area will not insert itself into my being and force me to forget my stern roots of New England, which has made me who I am: a man of strong convictions and a sturdy sense of right and wrong. And, thank God, an Episcopalian.

*   *   *

However--I do enjoy seeing my name on the parish letterhead:

St. Swithun's Episcopal Church

29 Winchester Street, West Banana Bay, Florida 32174

PArkway 3-7300

and right below that:

George Oliver Dudley, Rector, D.D., D. Min., M. Div.

Take *those* letters, Mr. Leland Frye, B.A.!

My mother named me before telling my father. She says she had me baptized secretly in the hospital before he could find out, warning the skeptical visiting priest with the vial of holy water that I was premature (at eight pounds!) and might not survive the night. She had already determined that I would be a priest myself, and that is why she gave me my name with the initials G.O.D.

It looks very smart stamped in gold on my leather briefcase. G.O.D. *Very* smart.

Few people can claim that their mothers are true saints. My mother is one. I am certain she only had intercourse one time and that was to conceive me. She suffered and endured all through her married life with my father, who tended to tipple some after work. How he would laugh when she and I used the word "tipple". (We two had private jokes like that.)

"Rhymes with 'nipple', of which I ain't seen one of yours in years, Holy Doris, Mother of *G.O.D.!*" he'd roar, while she put her finger to her lips and cast looks of disapproval toward the coat closet, where she had hidden me until we could catch what kind of mood he was in.

He repaired cars for a living. The oily-gaseous smell of his work clothes permeated our house, even after he was alive one minute and dead the next from a massive heart attack. To this day, when I have to ride in Mrs. Hitchcock's car and smell the diesel fumes, it is all I can do to keep from panting, grabbing the door handle and heaving myself outside onto the prickly St. Augustine grass.

I was not at home when he died. I was at college, studying theology and singing in the chapel choir. It was my mother who told me about my father's death: "Now, George, a dead person just doesn't look the same as a live one, because the soul's gone out of him or her. But your father, may he rest in peace, looked the same alive *and* dead."

Did she mean he had no soul? Oh, that could not be! Every person on the face of this earth surely had a soul. Even Hitler—well, I am sure he *had* one, I mean, he was once a baby himself, although as he got older he had that awful trademark hair-comb and little mustache, so that today if you happen to see someone dressing like that, you can just *know* he is up to no good; but Hitler sold his soul to the Devil for the empty promise of world domination.

Odd how "domination" and "damnation" look so alike.

So then did his soul go straight to hell or did it go to heaven first, where God got to sit on His throne frowning in judgment while the millions of dead Jewish and military people and European homeless were allowed to castigate him for his wanton devastation?

I am supposed to know these things, because I am a priest and a man of the cloth. Do any other clergy people wrestle this way?

In high school Mr. Burns, our history teacher asked, "If white is good and black is bad, then what is most of life?"

The entire class called out, "Black! Black!" or "White! White!" while I was still making up my mind. (Their raucous spontaneity always tended to derail my reasoning ability.)

"Grey," he said. "Most of life is grey."

No! I thought. That cannot be. Things either *are* or they are *not*. No in-between! When I become a priest, I promised myself, I will *never* preach an in-between grey philosophy.

Did Jewish people go to heaven? (I needed another drink of Scotch while thinking about this.) I figured it just depended on their beliefs. But surely, if they believed wrong and not in Jesus, that would not keep them out. Just because someone does not believe in a private country club, that does not mean that one does not exist.

          *   *   *

It is perhaps a rankling issue that I have not been invited to join the exclusive Banana Bay Yacht Club and Golf Course. The only time I get to go there is when one of the parishioners invites me, and always for lunch and not dinner. I try to still the thought that it might be because of my new wife's sometimes dubious social skills that I am not invited as often as I would prefer.

I began this journal because of Gail, my wife. It is as though my life cleaved itself like the parting of the Red Sea into two parts: Before Gail and After Gail. And now—is there to be an After **After** Gail? I dare not look into that future.

*   *   *

I keep my journal locked and the key around my neck, under my collar. Of course with Gail's having run away with Leland Frye, there is no need to hide anything—I am alone here in the rectory. Gail gone, Mother gone, Gail's daughter Amber gone, Leland gone—all of them disappeared (well, at least I know where Mother and Amber are—in Mother's high-rise apartment) without a thought as to what this is doing to me!

Despite myself I have to smile: in this part of Florida I have learned that a "high-rise" has all of six floors. Mother is on the top floor of hers. I am cautious about her elevator. Too many retired people living there are jabbing away at the buttons on every floor and might tend to freeze it up while I am in it alone and no way to call for help. I hold my breath in the elevator every time.

I would take the stairs—probably good physical fitness; but at my advancing age of almost 40 I do not dare chance a heart attack, even though I am in rather good shape and only slightly overweight. But to die on the stairs which no one uses, alone, unable to call for help?

No. I would rather hold my breath and take the elevator.

Ordinarily I hide the key at night beneath the undershirt I wear to bed. To prevent people from asking about the book I have labelled it "A Comprehensive and Exhaustive Study of the Earliest Churches in the Western Hemisphere named St. Swithun's, translated from Early Anglo-Saxon".

That should be enough to keep idle eyes away. Also, alone, I am not forced to hide my taking a little nip now and then. Just to calm my nerves. So much on my plate!

I met Gail at J.C. Penney's, merely a month after Mother and I had settled in here. (Hm-m. Was I drawn there by the initials J.C.? Jesus Christ? Did Christ *Himself* lead me into Gail's life, knowing that she needed to be saved, along with her daughter Amber, from a "slipping down life"?) It was the day after Labor Day.

 She was working there in the men's department—why, I do not know to this day. More work of the Lord, perhaps—and although I had gone in to buy underwear, I found myself too embarrassed in her presence to discuss such a personal matter. I made a hasty exit and drove to K-Mart instead, where I hoped parishioners would not see me purchasing such inexpensive briefs. Mother should have been doing this for me, but she was off in St. Cloud visiting her aging aunt Flora just when I needed her home with me, where she belonged.

Necessity urged me back the next day to Penney's, since I knew their shorts fit better than the ones from K-Mart, which kept riding up.

At least I had only bought one package of them. The K-Mart underwear went right into the BOX FOR THE POOR.

I really wanted a salesman to help me, but there she was again. Her badge read "Gail" and she had a large smile, nice teeth and blonde hair that was cut like June Allyson's in the old 1940's movies. This time I put aside my shyness and went directly to the shelves with the briefs. Out of the corner of my eye I saw her approach me.

"Father," she said, and her voice made it sound as though we were conspirators. "Father, there's a sale starting Friday on these. Buy one package and get one at half price."

"Oh! I am sorry—I cannot get away then."

"I could—hold them for you. Until you could get back to the store. The sale price would still be good."

I blushed furiously at the idea of her holding my Jockeys.

She nodded as though I had agreed. "Just tell me what size, and they're yours." She brought a pencil from her breast pocket and I was forced to notice how perky and full her chest was.

'Yep, that's my name on my badge." She tapped it with a bright green fingernail.

"Oh—I am sorry. Did not mean to stare like that. It is just—well, uh, other people spell that name with a 'y' or an 'le', or. . . "

"How do I spell your name, Father? So I can set these aside?"

I could not tell if she was laughing at me or not. I gave her my card, the one with the prominent Episcopal logo on it. When she took it I glanced at her left hand: an immense cheap fake ruby , but no wedding ring She was as tall as I, so I altered my gaze—incredibly high heels! How did she *walk* in those things?

So she must be five feet five inches. I am used to telling myself that I am five feet seven and three-quarter inches. There is something old-fashioned in me that believes the man should always be taller and older than the wife . . . what was I *doing*, fantasizing about her as my wife?

But it was true. I suddenly realized that I wanted a wife. Standing in the middle of the men's department at J.C. Penney's, I wanted a wife. I wanted someone who would say to me, "George, you need new underwear. I'll pick you up some the next time I'm in the mall. No, no, of course I won't get the K-Mart ones. I know how you are."

It had been my clear assumption when I came as a bachelor a little over a month ago at age 39 to St. Swithun's that single women would be flattered to go out with me, given my title and position. But somehow they sensed that I had been at liberty too long, so that a kind of musty untried odor emanated from me. Maybe (although I doubted this strongly) I was getting set in my ways. Maybe my (what I had thought of as a Christian asset) virginity gave off some kind of aura. At any rate, no covey of smiling younger women had yet stood around at the Sunday after-church coffee hour, glancing at me and then nodding to each other, casting lots in their own secret ways to decide who would be the one to woo me.

Only the coy nasal Agnes Brown had shown any subtle romantic interest toward me, and she looked older than I, with a hint of downy mustache. She also stood too close to me when she chatted.

"Father? What size?"

I started. "Uh—I appreciate your help," I stuttered.

"Part of my job," she said, and moved away smiling. I noticed that she had a slight limp. A birth defect? A touch of polio as a child?

It was-- endearing. To use an old-fashioned word: I was smitten.

*   *   *

When Gail showed up for choir rehearsal a week later I was taken by surprise, especially since I was on hand in the music room/parlor to give the choir a pep talk about the proper way to walk up the aisle. "Do not even *try* to sing parts while you are walking," I said with my practiced chuckle, to set them at ease. "Just sing the melody line. I do not want you tripping on your way to the choir stalls."

Miss Peabody scowled. But then she always scowled. An unhealthy large dumpy combination organist and choir director at age 83, I had inherited her along with the church. She had been here since the church was built and no one dared oppose her.

"She knows where all the bodies are buried," Mrs. Hitchcock had murmured to me once. Well, she ought to—she had played for more burial services than I would possibly officiate at during my lifetime. "She and Edith Hatcher were rivals for the same man."

Miss Harriett Peabody directed the choir from the organ bench. This made both her directing and her playing somewhat spotty, and it annoyed me each Sunday that it appeared the little choir was singing to Miss Peabody and not to God.

And then not three months after my arrival at St. Swithun's, chance occurred in the form of Cat-Mandoo, who roamed freely around the neighborhood (hence the ever-present fleas on the poor cat's body). Mrs. Gustafson, who lived down the street from the church, had been politely requested to keep the cat inside, but Mrs. Gustafson was a Child Of Nature, once even wandering outside by herself without a stitch on as her dotage increased.

And that is how Miss Peabody ended up face down on the church lawn, squashing the unfortunate Cat-Mandoo as that feline chased squirrels up the water oaks in front of the parish hall. Miss Peabody broke a wrist and an elbow. The five choir members who were lagging behind after choir rehearsal heard a stream of invective emanate from the venerable organist, the likes of which they did not think she knew.

I visited her in the hospital. I do not relish going to hospitals. I know it is said that the staff scrub so that there are no germs, but they cannot check every latent-diseased visitor! For example, Miss Peabody: sitting across from her bed was a tall aging cowboy, of all things, his hat in his lap, and who knew what infections he had brought with him from a barn!

I took our organist's plump good hand, murmured a prayer, made the sign of the Cross and a hasty exit, stopping only at a sanitizer dispenser on the wall to wash my own hands.

So God moved in mysterious ways. Miss Peabody of course had to be replaced immediately and a private ceremony held for Cat-Mandoo; and soon afterwards I secured the promise of pipe organ money from the quavering, too-naked Mrs. Gustafson. Her ashes soon mingled with her cat's in the hallowed burial ground behind the church.

The door opened and there Gail was, smiling as if she knew her way. "A new choir member!" exclaimed Mrs. Hitchcock in her vibrato voice which never changed whether she sang or talked, which was often. "Are you a soprano or an alto?"

"Actually, I'm a soprano, but I can sing alto if you need. I read music pretty well. I used to sing in a band, see, and we travelled all over--maybe you heard of it: 'Gail and the'--"

"Ah. Well, sit here next to me in the soprano section. That will make two of us. I'll show you the ropes. And your name is--?"

"Gail Grace." She gave me a shy smile: see, I know how to act in front of your congregation. I would never cause you any embarrassment or gossip.

Oh, I thought and my heart actually leapt. Gail Grace. Gail Grace. Amazing Grace. And she became, just seven weeks from then, my own Amazing Gail Grace Dudley. Mrs. George Dudley.

Oh, thank you, Lord for underwear and Jesus Christ Penney's.

I was therefore astounded to discover that Gail came with baggage in the form of a sulky fourteen-year-old daughter named Amber Grace. When I found out about Amber I decided then and there that Gail would have to be a young widow, grieving over the loss of her husband in the Afghan war. I could not imagine that anyone in the parish would bother to check on Afghanistan. Of course they would accept my story—from a priest!

No one checked. Good thing, too, because Gail, of course, behaved much more like a merry widow than a sad one.

"George," Gail sat on the arm of my leather chair and ruffled my hair, which I found to be quite a pleasant feeling despite my having to work on my sermon. "Would it hurt your standing in the church if people knew I was a single Mom?"

"And that is the last time you shall say those words to me, or to anyone else."

She plopped herself lightly into my lap, creasing my notepaper. "Okay. I don't know where he is, anyway. He might *be* dead, for all I know. I never told him he was gonna be a father—"

"*Please*, Gail. Let me adopt Amber and that will be an end to it. And do say 'going to' instead of 'gonna'. All right?"

In the end I did not formally adopt Amber. We would have had to dig into her natural father's past and I was reluctant to do so, although Gail in some excitement looked upon it as a game, like that of Cat-Mandoo going after squirrels.

And so it was. I believe Amber reluctantly accepted me as her stepfather. The three of us walked down the aisle together when Gail and I wed. Gail was six years younger than I, and two inches shorter without her heels, which I persuaded her to give up. Everything pointed to a happy marriage. I was just sorry that Mother had to miss the wedding. She phoned from her aunt's in St. Cloud and said she was down with a sick headache and could not drive home.

We asked the organist from St. Barnabus to play for the service, since we were still attempting to find one to replace Miss Peabody. This should have been my first clue that God Himself was trying to prevent this union, let alone Mother's absence. How selfish I was, not to include Mother! But Gail and I had shared—a carnal experience, and I felt the need to make everything *simpatico* in the eyes of our Lord. Also I had promised

Our Lord that I would not do, uh—that—again with Gail until after the wedding.

For a moment I had considered postponing the ceremony until Mother came home. If only, if only . . . Ah, God forgive this weak flesh of mine! All the fault of Florida, Lord. You know that—all the fault of Florida. No need down here to bundle up in coat and scarf, no need to hide the female form, no need to dash in from the stormy blast—people here seem to *love* to stand outside and talk! I did not find that kind of idleness in New England, as far as I was able to tell. People up there have better things to do than to lounge around on the beach!

I am not blaming You, Lord. It is that down here things seem to move faster than in Connecticut. Perhaps it is the propinquity to the Space Center and rockets hurtling up beyond the speed of sound. Or the rootlessness—I certainly know that down here *I* felt rootless until I met Gail. Oh!-- falling in love with Gail! . . . Oh, Lord and oh Mother, forgive me for my fleshly failings.

All because of the chair leg in the bar

> "O O O O That Shakespeherian Rag—
>
> It's so elegant
>
> So intelligent"
>
> T.S. Eliot: The Waste Land

Gail's feet hurt. Too much dancing the night before—what a stupid thing to do, celebrate *Labor Day!*-- and that huge guy who bragged how light he was on his feet had stepped hard onto one of hers, so that she was limping a little today. Damned cocksure males!

At least her head didn't hurt too. She sighed. Every time she worked in the men's department at Penney's she knew she was in for a long afternoon. They always came in couples, the women picking out the underwear or shirts while the men just nodded like dazed little boys. The whole thing was boring!

She looked at her hands, admiring her "Jungle Vixen Green" nail polish and the imitation ruby she'd bought at such a huge discount, just because she was an employee here! Wait. Did the combination make her look too much like *Christmas?* She fretted, but just for a moment.

Well, at least she could play her game to pass the time. Her rules were simple: the third man she waited on she was going to marry. Teenagers and kids didn't count. Her game had given her many laughs in years past, as she worked passing out drinks in bars, singing in the band, cleaning up food spills in restaurants, making change as a cashier. She'd picture life with every third man. They never knew why she was smiling or looking pained.

At least this job was a step up, although the hours were erratic. Gail glanced around. There were no men approaching her. To play, she'd have to find *them*.

But first she had to navigate around a gaggle of adolescent girls, fresh from school and with nothing on their minds except experimenting with makeup, trying on clothes and discarding them in heaps on the dressing room floor, then whipping out their daddies' credit cards, while flashing those perfect brace-filled teeth and never a glance at the one who was tidying up after them.

I probably look like an old lady to them, Gail thought. *And Amber could be one of them, except without a credit card of her own father's. And I'm thirty-three and what the hell do I have to show for it, except a Penney's badge, a teenage daughter who barely tolerates me, and DeeDee—damn, what a self-centered roommate I found, bringing trashy scary men home to our apartment. I've got to somehow get a better life for us!*

As if her thoughts of disgust about DeeDee were written on her face, one of the teenagers glanced at her and then whispered to another and they both laughed. Pushing and shoving in a good-natured way, the cheerleader-like group headed for Sephora and an afternoon of magenta eye shadow trials and more giggling.

The laughter pulled Gail back to the reality of the men's department and her game. She stepped into the main aisle. "May I help you?" she asked a pleasant-looking man about her age, thirty or so. He gawked at her.

A woman rushed up to him, grabbed his arm and hurried him away, narrowing her eyes at Gail and frowning as she did so. "I told you to meet me in *purses*, Harry," she hissed.

Okay. That was *one*, for better or worse. And here came an old man with a cane! Well, he had to count as number two. And all he wanted was handkerchiefs! Did anyone even *sell* those anymore? He'd be much better off with tissues. But he was so grateful for her help that she patted him gently on one of his bony shoulders and sold him a box of handkerchiefs autographed with a "W". So far, the high spot of her day.

William? Weevil? Woodrow? My god, was she *that* bored?

She looked down at her wristwatch. Great! Only twenty minutes to go! Maybe take home Burger Kings, although Amber had complained about the lack of home cooking and Gail had challenged her, sarcastically, to try cooking something herself, after which they had both retreated to opposite ends of the tiny apartment, like battle-weary boxers—maybe Burger King, yes—and then she looked up and one row over from her was her third man.

A priest. She laughed to herself. Damn! A Catholic priest with a collar! Wasn't that just her luck!

He was holding a package of underwear and looking rather absently at it.

"Father," she said. He looked at her then, startled out of his plastic bag contemplation, and she nearly gasped at the blueness of his eyes. Paul Newman blue! He was her height, so that she was able to stare directly into those terrific eyes without craning her neck. A little overweight, but what a nice face! His complexion was ruddy, or maybe he was blushing. This idea pleased her: a man *blushing*--!

"Uh—excuse me," he stammered and dropped the package into her hands. And fled.

Well, so much for *that* marriage. She forgot about him as soon as he was out of her sight.

He was back the next day. She'd been out dancing again after they'd eaten their hamburgers; Amber had gone to study for a test; and DeeDee had promised she would let no men into the apartment—"I have to wash my hair *sometime*, you know!" DeeDee had snapped--

and this time while Gail was sitting (doing nothing else than sitting!) at a table in the bar at the Banana Bay Inn, some man had pulled up a chair and sat down next to her, and one of the chair legs had landed squarely on her foot. Oh, the pain had been unbearable! "Damn it all to hell!" Gail had yelled.

"Oh, my god, I'm so sorry! Did I break anything? Oh, shi--are you okay? Can I take you to the hospital? Get an x-ray?"

"She'll be okay," said his apparent date, muscling herself into a place at the little table and scowling at Gail. The woman's teeth were nicotine yellow and she looked ready for a fight.

"I'll be okay," Gail agreed, walking around, trying the foot to see if she could put any weight on it. God, did that hurt! But she wasn't going to get into a stranger's car, especially with that angry girlfriend, and she wasn't going to pay for any damned emergency room bill. She'd wised up to that fast years ago with her daughter Amber.

"Father," she said now. She wasn't even counting men today, so she had no idea if he was her third or thirty-third customer. "Back for underwear?"

Oh, he *was* blushing! His eyes were still that beautiful shade of blue, so clear and innocent, and he had an almost girlish set of eyelashes. His pleasant face was wide-open and innocent. She reminded him about the sale and he handed her his card.

Oh! An Episcopal priest! *They* could marry, right? She stared at the card.

"See my initials?" the priest said, pointing. His fingernails were so polished! Did his wife do that for him? She read: George Oliver Dudley. G.O.D.

"Oh!" Gail laughed. "Oh, that's funny!"

He frowned.

"I mean *clever*! Very creative! Did you make it up yourself? Do people call you 'Ollie'? "

"Mother named me. And *no*. Never."

Mother. Not "my mother". Huh. Maybe he wasn't a real priest, but belonged to some sect on the outskirts of religion. Was that what—uh—Episcopals were? A fringe group? With a Mother? Wait, though—if he was a Father, maybe that made his *wife* a Mother.

"My mother wanted me to be a priest from before I was born, and—here I am."

Oh. Okay. "My mother", not his wife. Gail turned the full force of her personality, which she knew she could do, since she had done it so many times in the past, on him.

"Yep. Here you are." She studied the card. "St. Swithun's. That's a—an unusual saint. Never heard of it. Where's your church?"

"It is on a short dead-end street near the causeway. The church itself is pretty old. Do you know where Winchester Street is?"

There was some hesitancy in his voice. Her face shone suddenly: "Oh! You mean that little *blue* church!"

"Blue. Yes, that is the one." He didn't seem overly pleased.

"Well, why didn't you *say* so? Everybody knows the *blue* church!" And Gail suddenly began to sing: "Am I blue, am I buh-loo? Are these tears in my eyes over yo-o-ou?"

She stopped, aware that he was regarding her as some exotic animal he'd just come across, and possibly dangerous.

"You—you have a very nice voice."

"Well, when I was in school—junior high *and* senior high-- I sang in the chorus for years. Even *solos*! And then in a real band! I got to wear the cutest outfits! 'Gail and the Gorillas'! People thought I looked like Fay Wray, she's an old actress, and the guys in the band were so big next to me they looked like King Kongs! I don't sing much lately, though. I feel really out of practice."

"I have heard of Fay Wray, yes. You do remind me a bit of her."

They regarded each other for a moment and then she said, "Uh--let me check at the register for you." Then she added, "I think I might need your driver's license also."

"Oh. Certainly. Of course." He fumbled with his wallet and handed her the plastic rectangle.

"Be right back. Don't go away. Not that you *could*. I have your driver's license, right?"

She was glad she'd washed her hair this morning and she flipped her head into the air to make the blonde pageboy bounce. She tried not to limp as she walked away from him. The area on the top of her foot was already turning purple and she'd had a hard time putting on heels this morning.

Once her back was to him, she looked at the license. Birthdate—that made him—uh, thirty-nine. Six years older than her. That wasn't bad. His photo certainly didn't show off his eyes. And he wanted to have his organs donated. Good-- a sign that he wasn't selfish.

She had no idea what was happening to the man watching her walk away. As if she'd pierced his heart with an arrow of love, she could not have done more to smite the suddenly defenseless George Oliver Dudley, D.D., D. Min., M. Div. with that little limp—her David's stone a straight shot to his Goliath's head.

"Father, these are going to be on sale on Friday. Buy one package and get another package at half price-"

He moved a step closer to her then and held out his hand—to hold hers?

"My license, please."

She gave it to him, making sure that their fingers touched. She watched his eyes dilate.

She appraised him swiftly—could he be marriage material, even for a priest? She needed to be true to the rules of her little game. He *had* to count as number three, even if that was from yesterday. His breath smelled nice. She hoped the onion rings from last night hadn't hung onto hers.

She secretly checked his left hand. No wedding ring. *Wait*—maybe he was gay. Weren't a lot of clergymen gay these days? Or was that just the Catholic Church? They should be *ashamed* of themselves, going after young boys and getting them liquored up by making them drink sacramental wine! That's what DeeDee said. She had told Amber she herself was a lapsed Catholic, which meant she went to confession to get absolution, so she could keep bringing men home without guilt. Until the next confession. Damned DeeDee! She had a revolving door of men coming to their place.

DeeDee. Another weird mouth-breathing man had entered their apartment last night, so that Gail and Amber had locked their bedroom door from the inside just in case.

"But Mom, dammit, what if I have to go to the bathroom?"

"I'll go with you. And what did I tell you about swearing?"

"I'm not a *baby*." Amber had looked relieved and accusing at the same time. "How long are we staying here? DeeDee keeps using my shampoo."

Oh, she really had to get them out of there. Gail hated to leave her teenager alone in that place. It just wasn't right. Or safe. Or even maybe legal. At the thought of some government agency swooping in and taking a terrified protesting Amber away, Gail's heart constricted. She must not let that happen!

Father George Oliver Dudley—G.O.D. to her now (*His mother must have quite the sense of humor!* Gail thought) shifted from one foot to the other. "Well. I must be going."

"Nice meeting you. I'll save you two pairs of underwear. Maybe *blue* ones, to match your church." Now they both blushed and he backed away so fast that he stumbled into a dummy modeling a suit.

"Thank you. Very kind of you," he muttered to the dummy. And he was gone.

Gail could hear the teenaged girls screaming in laughter from across the store. Mrs. George Dudley, she tried it out. Gail Grace Dudley. G.G. D.-- Good Grief Doc. Good

Gravy Daddy. Green Glass Doggy. Yeah, that was a good one. Gorgeous God Damn. Nah.

My god! Would she have to learn how to pour *tea*? Were Episcopals allowed to go out dancing and *drinking*? She'd better do some religion research before she played her third man game again.

Two visions entered her mind at the same instant—his blue eyes and Amber's accusing ones.

"Say, Janice," she called to a woman at the register. "What do you know about Episcopals?"

III. George's Bird and Church are Blue—the Color, not the Song

> "The Child is father of the Man;
>
> And I could wish my days to be
>
> Bound each to each by natural piety."
>
> William Wordsworth: My Heart Leaps Up When I Behold

I found a bird in the road when I was, I believe, nine years old. We were living in Connecticut and there were not many houses around us, so there were not many neighbors or children my age to play with. I spent many hours by myself, either reading or sitting in the kitchen with Mother while she cooked.

(Yes, that is correct: I was nine. Ordinarily I would have been entering fourth grade, but my intellectual prowess had shifted me up one year, so that I was going to be a fifth grader in the fall.)

"Go outside, George. I've got a lot to do before your father gets home." She lifted the lid of a pot on the stove and a billow of steam made her blink.

"I can just sit here and be quiet."

"George—"

"I could watch TV." "Rocky and Bullwinkle" were not on yet, I knew. Most of the humor eluded me about the moose and the flying squirrel—they talked so fast!—but that did not matter. My favorite part of that show was Dudley Do-Right of the Canadian Mounties, who with his horse galloped around rescuing the fair Nell from a slimy scoundrel who kept tying her up.

We had the same name, Dudley! Oh, I yearned to—what? Own a horse? Save a fair maiden? The only maiden I knew was Mother; I was too shy to talk to any of the girls in class. Besides, they were all taller and louder than I was and did not seem to be in any immediate need of rescuing.

"George Oliver, I just can't concentrate with you in the house. I can't keep answering your everlasting questions and keep my mind on my work at the same time."

I could see that I would not be able to think of a good enough reason to stay by her side, so I went out, shutting the screen door without a bang so that she could realize what a good obedient son I was being; and that is when I found the bird.

Mother would not let me bring it inside. "They have germs. And besides, this one's almost dead. Nothing you can do about it. Now don't you start crying, with your father coming home. You know how he hates that."

I was not about to cry. I decided I was going to give this poor unfortunate bird last rites and a funeral. Because was it not true that I going to be a priest when I grew up? This was something real to practice on.

"May I have a glass of water, Mother?"

"George, for heaven's sake, get it yourself. I can't be waiting on you all the time."

I procured a glass of water—"One of my *best* glasses, George? My land!"-- and a few strips of paper towels. "In case I spill," I explained to her, although she had not asked. I hoped she would see how good I was being, to make up in advance for whatever mood Father would be in when he got home.

Outside, I wrapped the bird in the paper towels and poured some water onto its head. It was not moving at all by now and its eyes had a funny look. "I forgive you all your sins," I said in the most solemn voice I could speak. Then I made the sign of the Cross, as I had been taught. But what sins would a *bird* have committed?

As I knelt, a rain of gravel bounced off my back.

"Whatcha doin', Duh-Duh-Dudley?" Two boys from my class stood too near to me to allow me to hide the bird. I looked up: Lefty and Spunky. I knew their names, but nobody except the teacher ever called them by their real ones—Emmett and Warren. They lived three streets over, although staying in their own territory was never one of their problems.

"I --found a bird—"

"No kiddin'." Both boys now hovered over my bird and the bigger one, Emmett, stooped down and picked it up.

"No! My mother says germs--!"

"Germs! Ya scared of *germs*?" The bird was thrust into my face. I tried to hold my breath, but could not. I inhaled the dustiness of it and coughed.

"Let's see if this thing can still fly!" and with that he threw the hapless bird into the air, as though it were a football. I watched in dismay as it landed in a lilac bush at the edge of the next neighbor's yard.

"Got anything else, Georgie-porgie?" He picked up Mother's glass, dumping out the water all over my head.

"No! That's my mother's! Don't break it!"

"I wasn't gonna *break* it, you twerp! I was gonna *throw* it!" And with that he heaved the glass in the same direction. I marked where it fell so that I could retrieve it when they were gone.

The smaller boy, Warren, who was still bigger than me since, as I had mentioned, I had skipped a grade the year before with Mother's blessings and pride, now stared at me. "Hey, Spunky—see if you can throw Georgie-porgie, too."

But I dodged past him and onto our front porch and into the house, banging the screen door as I did.

"George? What are you doing?" Mother looked at my heaving chest and scrunched-up face and strode fast to the front porch. "You boys get out of here! Don't let me see you in my yard again!"

The two boys grinned at her, unabashed. Now I would have to face them in school, and who knew what would happen to me without Mother there?

"Where's my glass, George?"

"Oh. Outside."

"Those things don't grow on trees, you know." And she returned to the kitchen.

I scrubbed my face, brushed my teeth to get rid of bird germs, then waited until I was sure Spunky and Lefty had gone. I went searching for the glass and the bird. I found both of them easily enough. The bird was dead. Happily, the tumbler was intact, although dirty. I dug a little hole, using the glass, then pushed the bird into the hole with my foot. I then covered it up and sprinkled the mound with some aromatic lilacs, checking all the while to make sure the neighbor or the boys did not come around to see what I was doing.

I could not determine whether to cry or get angry. In the end I did neither. I said a prayer for the blue bird and then I forced myself to say a prayer for Spunky and Lefty—that they would see the error of their ways and straighten out properly and mostly leave me alone on the school playground.

"Lord, I know you made them as well as me, but I am having a hard time believing You are someday actually going to let *them* into the same heaven I am going to."

Then I said another prayer, a fervent one that I would not die from inhaling bird germs.

"Dust to dust, ashes to ashes," I whispered. I heard a car door slam. "And God, please protect us from Father." The prayers for the dead were finished; now I needed some for the living: "Lord, I need him in a good mood so I can watch Dudley Do-Right."

*   *   *

I answered the invitation (how green and untried I was!) to my first parish on the other side of Connecticut, many miles and years from where I had buried that bird. I had wondered in amusement if that bird had chirped a prayer to God that I wanted to stay in my home state.

But then Mother's arthritis acted up and the cold winters became more than she could bear, so when a call went out from a little Episcopal church in a place called Banana Bay, Florida—Mother and I had never been south of Bridgeport!—we talked it over and prayed about it and I decided to send them my name and profile.

I was especially interested in leaving Connecticut, since the Episcopal Church here seemed to be growing more and more liberal. My choir was demanding praise music! I was not sure how long I could hold them off from what I considered to be camp songs like "Kum-ba-yah". And the parish in the next town over had just hired a self-proclaimed *homosexual* priest, to my discomfiture. Would I be able to shake his hand at meetings?

"It's a pretty enough church—look, George," Mother exclaimed over the photos I had been sent. "Stained glass, white clapboard siding—why, it could be right at home here!"

She was so excited about being "next door to my Aunt Flora!"—we did not yet know how far apart the distances in Florida are—that I pursued the matter. The boy who mowed the church lawn came into my office at my request to find St. Swithun's on the internet—I was not sure how to do that and did not want to break any church equipment (I certainly could not ask a church member to check on a rival parish), but he came up short.

"Nope. Looks like there's no website for this church."

"Oh, well, I guess I will not use that name in my research," I said, in what I thought was a necessary prevarication so he would not spread any gossip.

It was not until the phone interviews were completed months later—St. Swithun's could not afford to fly me down there for a face-to-face interview and both of us could not have afforded plane tickets (there was no way I was going to leave Mother alone while I basked by myself in the Florida sun), and I had been accepted as their new rector sight unseen, and we had packed and driven down in my used but dependable sedan (this was August—I made sure the air conditioning worked), that we discovered I had become the new rector of a *blue* church. Not pale blue, either—this was an all-out, in-your-face bright blue. It glistened in the bright Florida sun. Now I had of course never seen a house of ill repute, but if one were to be painted, I was sure it would be this color.

"George!" Mother gasped. I stared. Where was the neat white clapboard? The little house next door was also blue—the same shade. All right: *one* building—that could have been a painting error. But then to go ahead and do it *again*--?

*   *   *

"It was that terrible Edith Hatcher," exclaimed Mrs. Gladys Hitchcock, opening and shutting doors and checking for dust as she escorted us through our new blue rectory home. "That's your bedroom and bath, Mrs. Dudley, and over here is your bedroom and—uh, bath."

Mrs. Hitchcock reddened at having to show me anything porcelain. She was around Mother's age, I guessed, and also a widow. Apparently she was the Welcoming Committee.

"Edith Hatcher was a mean person—sorry, Father, but she *was*—and when Miss Peabody—she's our organist, you'll meet her, she looks grim, but don't you worry—where was I? --oh yes, her oldest and dearest friend, found her will written in the back pages of Edith's Bible twenty-odd years ago, Edith Hatcher had written that the church must be painted blue in perpetuity—I think that's the right word. Oh, my."

She wiped her forehead. Mother and I did the same to ours. "You get used to sweating here in Florida. The AC will cool this place down pretty fast. It's a new one, installed just in time for you. Don't know how the early settlers did it. I guess their shoes just rotted right off their feet."

I sat down in a well-used leather chair in the den. Moist, I stuck to the leather, but decided that this would be *my* chair. A man's chair. A priest's chair. I pictured myself seeing parishioners in this room and helping them with their problems and then a prayer, then a pleasant glass or two of Scotch after seeing them out. Yes. This would do.

The two older women beamed at me in unison from the doorway.

"But," Mother continued the conversation, "that can't be *right*, that one person could have such a say over a thing like painting a church—"

"Well, our vestry every year votes to take it to court, but then we realize we don't have the money to do that, so we just put up with the blue color. We thought her grandfather had only *donated* the land and the church, but it's hard to argue with the words of a will written in the back of a millionaire's personal Bible."

"But—you sent us a photo of a white church!" Mother was not going to let Mrs. Hitchcock off the hook.

"I know. It's an old photo, over thirty years old." Mrs. Hitchcock was looking flustered—how should she fib in front of her new priest? Apparently she decided to blame the dead.

"--And that dreadful Edith Hatcher ordered painters to come in and before we knew what had happened, they were painting our church! This was right after Miss Peabody had discovered the will in the Bible and shown it to us."

"But the rectory is *also* blue!"

"Yes, well—see, the painters had so much blue paint left over that they said they'd give us a very good deal on painting this house, too. So—well, at least they *match*. The house was a pinkish-salmony color before that and didn't look good at all next to the blue church, if you know what I mean. It made them look like one house for boys and another house for girls."

"But no sole person has a right to paint a church whatever he or she--!" I was overcome with a powerful need to protect my new parishioners.

"Edith Hatcher's family gave the land for it. Her grandfather, mostly. Apparently he simply doted on Edith. And then she was so *mean*--!"

"Excuse me, Gladys," interrupted Mother. "I'm afraid I must lie down. This heat—"

"You need some salt and a glass of water," said Mrs. Hitchcock firmly. She turned to me. "I'll tend to your mother. You go look around the property. The story can wait."

I obediently walked outside and looked around. The August air was stifling, as though God had baked it in an oven before sending it down to earth. What had I gotten us into? And I was wearing *black* in all this heat. I was rather dizzy myself from the constant barrage of Mrs. Hitchcock's warbly voice.

As I stood there I watched it suddenly rain across the street. My side of the street remained dry. Oh, what foreign kind of country had I brought my poor mother to? This place, Banana Bay, did not seem too-- civilized. Shoes that would rot? I sensed a need for more decorum. More order.

And no wonder there was no web-thing on the computer. They did not want anyone looking at a blue church. Well, there had to be a way out of this. No person, living or dead, man or woman, if wrong—and surely this Edith Hatcher was *wrong* to impose her will on innocent people—would get away with this. She had met her match in George Oliver Dudley, yes sir!

I was glad I had bought a pair of sunglasses. They were still not dark enough to hide that glaring color.

As it turned out I would have to wait for Thursday's choir rehearsal to get all the details as to why a blue church had been foisted on me.

IV. The History of the Blue St. Swithun's, as told by its Choir of Just Five Members, if you don't count the Organist

> "And the night shall be filled with music,
> And the cares that infest the day,
> Shall fold their tents, like the Arabs,
> And as silently steal away."
>
> William Wadsworth Longfellow: The Day Is Done

St. Barnabus' Church in Banana Bay is the one the wealthy Episcopalians attend, the ones who live on the beachside, across the causeway and the Indian River lagoon. After they have paid huge hurricane taxes to rebuild their mansions, should a hurricane or tsunami sweep the homes away, these good people get into their Cadillacs and BMWs to drive over the causeway to the mainland on Sunday mornings. And then to the Banana Bay Yacht Club for brunch.

(I can see that I am still irritated about the Yacht Club. I have yet to be invited there for Sunday brunch.

I hear it is quite a spread. Yes, I know I am conducting services at that time of day. But still--)

Back for a trifle to St. Barnabus' Church, which does not have a pipe organ, for all their money.

St. Swithun's is about to. (This part was not in the choir's vocal history, since Mrs. Gustafson and her cat had not yet died, but I needed to insert my role in this legend.)

My new church, St. Swithun's, began in Banana Bay as an offshoot of St. Barnabus'—a mission church. It eventually gathered enough moneyed/determined people of its own to form its own parish and pay its own priest, and was upgraded to being an independent church.

The name St. Swithun's was courtesy of Miss Edith Hatcher, whose family were cattle people, going back at least a century. It is hard to believe that this part of Florida contains major cattle ranches, but there it is.

"Edith Hatcher's grandfather sent her to England for an education. Oh, she *wanted* to go! She had a lot of ambition at a time when girls weren't supposed to have any," whispered the meek and trim Miss Elliott (alto). We all leaned in to catch her words.

"Tramp!" I thought I heard Miss Peabody, seated at the upright piano in the parish hall, say under her breath. Did she mean Miss Elliott? Oh, surely not! Miss Elliott presented a clean and tidy appearance. And such shiny hair!

"He sent her to St. Swithun's School for Girls in Winchester, Hampshire, England—"

"—where the school colors are shades of blue."

"For a time we tried to call ourselves 'Old Swithunites', but Edith Hatcher soon put a stop to *that*. Sent us a letter stating that only she, an authentic alumna, could be called that. And only by her fellow alumnae. Oh, she was a tough one about rules!" Old Mr. Campbell (tenor) slapped his knee.

"Do you remember the time we were getting ready to have the buildings repainted white and she sent us a letter full of paint samples?"

"All of them shades of blue!" Mr. Foster (bass) boomed in. I realized they would only need one bass with him around.

"That became our code—instead of swearing—sorry, Father—we'd just look at each other and say, 'Shades of Blue'!" Agnes Brown (alto) simpered at me.

Agnes continued, "She sent letters to Miss Peabody for years and years. Oh, hearing Miss Peabody read those letters to us-- it was like *storybook time* for us!" And here she *winked* at me!

"Well, but surely—," I attempted to detour any possible romantic overture from her.

"Surely not, Father," argued Mrs. Hitchcock (soprano). "She had pots of money—"

"Pots and *pots* of money!" Miss Elliott's eyes were wide.

"—and she left it all to the church—she wrote her will in her *Bible*, Father, so that's *impressive*, with the proviso that St. Swithun's would retain the old English spelling—"

"Yes, people try to correct me when I tell them that—"

"—and the additional proviso that the church would always be in her school colors—"

"Shades of blue!" the entire choir of five adults sang in unison, like a football chant.

"St. Swithun's Day is July 15th. We always have a huge celebration on that day."

"We all wear blue! Sorry you just missed this one. But there's always next year!"

"Well, the *rector* is allowed to wear just a blue ribbon or something—." Miss Peabody, the organist, who disliked gossip or anything that might approach fun, I came to discover, nevertheless wanted not to be left out. She sat now at the piano, her hind regions overflowing the piano bench, drumming the same measure of music over and over again with her right hand.

"There's a saying that if it rains on July 15th , it will rain for forty days," Mrs. Hitchcock stopped my rejoinder—"we know, we know, Father, that in the Bible 'forty days' simply means 'a long time'. But isn't this a nice tradition! I don't know of any other church that has one like this."

"We all raise our umbrellas, just for fun. And we all invoke St. Swithun with his chant."

Ah. Another chant.

"All of our desserts are colored blue!"

"Just wait until you see blue Jello with blue whipped cream!"

"We all go home with blue teeth and tongues!"

"Then there's an auction and the one who donates the most blue items for it wins a prize!"

And as if rehearsed, all the members of the choir except Miss Peabody rose, put their hands over their hearts, and recited together:

"St. Swithun's day, if thou dost rain,

For forty days it will remain;

St. Swithun's day, if thou be fair,

For forty days 'twill rain no more."

"But it does not even *rhyme*!" I cried out, overcome with the arrogance of People With Money and those weak-kneed who just Tended To Go Along.

"Tradition holds that St. Swithun was buried outside in the rain, not inside a cathedral, until many years after his death in 863 A.D."

"The Year of Our Lord, you know, Father," murmured Miss Elliott. "And later they took his bones and buried them in different places." Her eyes widened again. "And also his *head*--!"

"Yes, yes, he doesn't need to know all that."

"But he should be told the meaning of the *rectory* name," Miss Elliott replied, flushing slightly. (Inwardly I applauded this woman for prevailing.) "He *is* living there, after all."

"Oh. Of course. There's also the story of why the rectory is called 'Hyde Abbey'."

"Yes, yes, well, that can be for later." I tried to regain control of my now-unwieldy group. "Sounds like afternoon tea and ivy—"

"--instead of what it is, a regular C.B.S. house. Concrete block and stucco." Mrs. Hitchcock's vibrato was becoming more pronounced. "Hyde Abbey—that was Edith Hatcher's house at St. Swithun's all through her school years."

"Ah," I said.

"Oh, the *letters* she wrote us! Well, not to us. She called us 'peons' in one of them. Actually, she wrote them to her best friend Miss Peabody here, who would come and share them with us. It was almost as though we were there with her!"

"Dukes and earls from all around pursued her, but she said no to them all. Isn't that right, Miss Peabody?"

Miss Peabody sniffed dramatically.

"When she finally came back here, she refused to ride a horse the way her grandfather had taught her. She rode with an English saddle for the rest of her life. Right, Miss Peabody?"

The organist suddenly slammed down the lid to the piano keys. "I think we've heard enough about Edith Hatcher. She was a *bully*. Please open your hymnals to number 470. Father George, will you join us?"

So we all left the "blue" conversation and sang a rousing (to me somewhat short-handed, considering the few choir members) rendition of "There's a wideness in God's mercy".

"Miss Peabody told us that she and Miss Hatcher were after the same man, you know," explained Miss Elliott to me as I walked her to her car after rehearsal. I sighed. I could see I already had a stalwart friend in this sweet woman. She and I discovered we had graduated from high school in the same year. What was her first name—Jocelyn? Rosalind? There were so many names to remember!

*   *   *

And all that is to let you know why, every morning when I raise my head from my solitary bed, I can glance through my window and tell, by the amount of sunshine bouncing off the eastern wall of the church, what the weather is like. I have plans to have a tree planted there, something wide-spreading, to minimize this diurnal eye-numbing sight. And secretly every morning I curse Edith Hatcher and her control over us all, even from the grave.

Even before I praise God for the new day, or urinate.

It is in Edith Hatcher's will, they have all told me, that the blue color remains until her money runs out. Which they also tell me is unlikely to happen any time soon.

It also explains where our street name of Winchester came from. Edith Hatcher must have, however grasping she was, genuinely loved that school.

*   *   *

Actually, the church is surprisingly pretty inside. It is more wide than it is high, so that it affords side aisles, as well as the center one. There are pews on either side of the center aisle, enough to seat, I estimate, one hundred fifty souls thirsty for the Word of God, three times as many than, I have been told, ever attend a service.

The stained glass windows are Victorian-sentimental but not garish. There are three long choir pews (the five or six choir members sitting there always looking rather abandoned) facing the small electronic organ from across the aisle up front, and there is a special chair for me when I am not standing at the pulpit or behind the homemade altar rail. There is a stained glass window at the front of the church over the altar, but so far I have not had the time to get a stepladder and climb up to make out the name of the donor. It is a rather recent addition and shows a saint, possibly St. Swithun himself, holding an orange. There is a palm tree on either side of him. Two horses stand at attention behind him. What odd Florida symbolism! I pray it is not anything pagan.

The place struck me from the start as having a pleasant oil of cloves odor, which I now understand is the smell of the furniture polish that Mrs. Hitchcock orders. (That woman must have her hand in all aspects of St. Swithun's.) The piano tuner visits the parish hall regularly and the organ is ancient, but a Baldwin, not a Hammond, for which I am grateful.

The rectory itself could use more closets, but the new AC pumps out cold air (thank you indeed, Lord), and the plumbing works. There are three bedrooms (four if you count my den), a living room ("A Great Room, Father, in Florida," said Mrs. Hitchcock) which encompasses a small dining area, sitting area and a view of the kitchen with its mismatched appliances, through an opening over the sink. The floors are terrazzo, apparently ground-up pieces of polished stone upon which anything dropped will break. ("Be sure to clean up mustard fast, Father, or it will soak right in and leave you a yellow stain.")

You will not have to take three guesses to discover my part-time secretary's name: yes, Mrs. Gladys Hitchcock. Miss Peabody, the organist, may know where the bodies are buried, but Mrs. Hitchcock juggles the needs of the living at a speed to make my head spin.

Which brings me to Mother.

Mother had always handled my front desk duties in Connecticut, filling in quite capably, so she was at a loss now in Banana Bay with Mrs. Hitchcock at the helm.

"George, I just don't know what to do with myself."

"What do you mean? You are my right *hand*. Why, I could not eat a meal without *you* in the kitchen. You know all my favorite foods."

"I know that, George, but . . ."

"But nothing! You are a man's best girl, you know that? This place would fall apart without you. Which reminds me—would you call the bug spray man again? I am still seeing ants in my den."

"George. Are you leaving dessert dishes in there? That will bring them faster than anything, especially down here. I'd better get in there and give the room a thorough going-over. And then *don't* eat in there—eat in the kitchen, where food belongs."

That lasted for less than a month. Then, out of nowhere:

"George. I've decided to take driving lessons."

"But why? You know I am happy to drive you wherever you want to go."

"Gladys Hitchcock drives and she's *my* age. She doesn't understand how I've gone all these years without driving. She's had *five* tickets for speeding! And I've never even sat behind the steering wheel of your car, even in the driveway. Her grandson Matthew's offered to teach me."

"But—we would need a second car!"

"Oh, pooh, George. You're here most of the time. It's not like you're out chasing fires. We could coordinate our schedules. Plus, your father used to let me drive without a license, with him in the car, when you were a baby. And my arthritis isn't acting up anymore!"

What was Mother doing, talking about *schedules*? She had never been this way in Connecticut. She had never needed a schedule—her routine was to be at my office when she was not at home cleaning and cooking, and then going to the supermarket once a week, sitting in the *passenger* seat, where a proper mother belonged.

"I'll just drive around the church parking lot at first, George. While you're working on your sermon."

Well, I could not think of a good defense. So the teenaged Matthew taught Mother to drive and while I refused to ride with her, with *me* in the passenger seat like a little child—I was not going to be seen in town with my *mother* driving me!—I had to admit watching her from a distance, that she seemed to take to it more easily than I expected.

"George—I think it would be a good idea if I had my own car."

"Mother! What are you saying?"

"I'm saying that Gladys Hitchcock's grandson Matthew can get me a good deal on a used car and I'm looking into it, George. Now get that sour expression off your face! I'm just *looking*!"

Four days later my father's retirement money was sitting in our driveway in the form of a 1999 black Toyota Corolla. "But low mileage, George." The word 'mileage' from my own mother!

Black. "It will be hot, Mother. I just do not know why you had to—"

But she was absorbed in polishing the hood with an old undershirt of mine. Her face had the sort of beatific glow you see on a Madonna in Rembrandt paintings. For a *car*!

I insisted on praying over her the first time she and Gladys Hitchcock drove to St. Cloud to visit Mother's aunt Flora, even though it was a straight shot on a back road with little traffic. "Next time I'm going to drive myself, all alone," she beamed.

I had never seen her like this! My dinners were late because she was out somewhere—she had managed to learn how to play bridge, of all things! "They need a fourth, George. I have to go." And sometimes *days* went by without my having fresh sheets on my bed. Florida was corrupting my mother and I needed to put a stop to it. But how?

Immediately she joined a group of women in church who were exercising and losing weight. "You could stand to lose a few pounds too, George." Odd new foods entered the house—Greek yogurt. Protein shakes. Hummus. "Mother, you know I am a steak and potatoes kind of man," I protested. Secretly, I had to admit she was looking more—healthy. Yes, that was it; she had gotten a kind of second wind, living down here. Tuesdays while I worked in my office, I could hear Jane Fonda's voice in the parish hall, along with the chuffing of a half-dozen females of various sizes and shapes. I avoided leaving my office at that time.

When I married Gail and brought her home, I fully expected the two dearest females in my life to bond together, their sole purpose to make my life easier. (I wasn't yet expecting Amber to bond—she was like a surly disapproving alien in my midst.)

I did not expect turf wars.

For a time, Gail obediently followed Mother around the kitchen. "See, Gail, this is how George likes his eggs."

"Hm-m-m," said Gail, cocking her head to one side. It would not hurt Gail to be taking notes, I thought, watching them. "But what if I do them with a little *butter*, the way I'm used to?" she asked brightly.

"I don't think so," replied Mother dubiously. She was still on a diet and I had not tasted that butter cake of hers since the choir party.

"C'mon, Doris. We'll each make 'em our way and then George can judge which one he likes best."

"Better," I said. "You are comparing two things, so it is 'better', not 'best'."

"Oh, George, you're so *cute* when you're smart!" and Gail plunked herself down on my unsuspecting lap, knocking my napkin to the terrazzo. Right in front of Mother!

"I'll just see if the paper's come," said Mother, leaving the room with a heavier tread than usual. "*And* you're wrinkling his good slacks. I just ironed them," she called back to her new daughter-in-law.

I had to admit the eggs that Gail made were very good. She even got me to try a cheese omelet with salsa, which I ate after much cajoling on her part, and asked for again the next day. Mother fortunately was not in the room. "Just please leave out the onions, Gail."

"Yeah, I've learned—onions make you fart! Whoo!"

"Gail--!"

Nights were—how can I describe this?—a mixture of heaven and hell. "Gail, could you please be a little quieter? With a little less moaning?"

"Huh? What? Was I being loud?"

"You are going to wake up everyone in the house, that is all," I whispered.

"Nah. Once Amber goes to bed, she's out like a light. C'mon, George, let me show you something—," and she slid under the sheet that my mother had just washed that day. Fresh and crisp—Mother always ironed them. Hm-m. Wait. She was not doing that anymore, since she had started playing bridge. I would have to get her to teach Gail about my sheets—

"Hey, lover, where'd you go? I'm not doin' this alone, you know!" And I'd return to this new untamed female in my life who was starting to lose patience with me.

This *is* difficult to explain, even in my journal, since I believe that—uh—relations between man and wife are sacred and private: but I had never been this close, this intimate with a woman before, and my fear of being heard from the other end of the house where Mother might be lying, sighing, praying for me, made me either "swelter" or "freeze"—no controllable in between.

(Not to mention—I had never had to worry about passing gas in bed with someone else there before.)

In other words, since to be honest I must place this part of my life also in my journal, I would either be-- unable to perform, or I would be so-- *fast* from start to finish that Gail was left behind.

Gail was aghast when she learned I had never had a serious girlfriend. "You mean, no fooling around, even a little bit? Even in high school? Even in college?"

"I had better things to do with my time," I answered sternly. "Like studying—"

"Okay, no more sermonizing, George. Lemme show you how it's done."

But it was no good. *I* was supposed to be in the driver's seat and *she* was to be the passenger, not the other way around. Had I not read manuals? I knew all the proper moves; but it was like reading a book on how to lift off in a rocket, to use a rather crass term. Nothing was like one expected just from reading a book. I was not prepared for such a *violent* lift-off.

I daresay that last paragraph will be understood without my having to write any more graphically, even though this journal is just for me.

I gathered by all that Gail knew, that she had had a rather active—former life. I did not know what to do about this. In a different culture, she would have had a ritual cleansing. I mentioned this once and she jumped out of bed, ran into the shower, and sang out in a voice I was sure Mother could hear, "I'm all soaped up in here, George. Come *cleanse* me!"

On the other hand, I *enjoyed* her so! I enjoyed her breath on my face, her eyes so close to mine, her fingers massaging my stressed shoulders, her hair hanging down on my cheeks, her firm skin next to my somewhat-flabby exterior—she gave herself so cheerfully to me!

Were *all* women this way, then? A discomforting image came to me: my father having relations with Mother, and more than *once*! And he so smelly and rough! No. Never!

I had to think more spiritually, to rid my mind of that image.

So--had Eve been like Gail way back in Eden—humorous, uncomplaining, able to make a joke about whatever came along, yet able to leap from smiling to being sober when the moment called for it; so passionate at night and so mindful of the business at hand during the day? It was good that God had made Eve, because Adam could never have believed he needed anyone else until this indispensable mate came along, so curious about that fruit, that store of knowledge.

Ah. Could it be? Might I have a topic for next Sunday's sermon here? It was not that the serpent tempted the innocent Eve—it was that the Creature *knew* that Eve would be the person more-- (not *most*, but more, a comparison of two—yes, I would bring a little teaching of grammar into my sermon, inserting it like a mental vitamin) --the more curious about knowing new things than the stolid Adam would.

Indeed, I was almost tempted to think that if God had made Eve first, He might not have bothered with Adam: and this was a rather troubling idea—what did Gail need *me* for?

She was changing me, this bride of mine! Changing my way of thinking, challenging my beliefs in her off-handed humorous way. What was happening to me? *The woman was supposed to be subject to the man!*

"Oh, I was subject to a man once before," Gail responded when I asked her to please try and think before she spoke, since I was in essence her new boss.

"See, and how did that go?"

"It resulted in *Amber*. No, I'm not going down that road again."

"But you are *supposed* to be subject to me! And the first time we met, you *limped!*"

"Don't you hold that against me, George. It was temporary, not permanent. Like *us,* if you keep this up!"

I ignored that. Perhaps I should not have.

"And, George-- *you're* supposed to be subject to *Christ*. My god, men *never* read that line. Being married doesn't mean that you're allowed to turn into a little dictator like Hitler. *And I don't limp!*"

That was our first argument. I could see that I was going to have to be more subtle. Yes, a soft word would turn away wrath. Reading her "The Song of Solomon" was of no help.

"A 'mound of *wheat*, George? You think my belly's a mound of wheat? You telling me I'm gaining *weight?*" And my Eve, subject to me only when she felt like it, ran to the bathroom scale.

Once I dared ask her. "Gail—what do you need me for?"

She looked up from the book she was reading and laughed. "First off, for a new outfit, George. The Swithunites are getting tired of seeing me in this one almost every Sunday."

"No, I mean—*please* do not call them Swithunites; we are not allowed to—seriously!—do you think they care about what you are wearing?"

"I can just tell you that Gladys Hitchcock offered to take me shopping! "

"But—what do you need me for?"

"George." And now her tone was serious. I heard her book hit the floor and then her arms were around me. "You take such good care of Amber and me. You're dependable. I always know where to find you. If I have a bad dream you comfort me. You're my rock. My cup runneth over with you, George."

Suspicious now, I picked up the dropped book. I should have known: "The Bible for Dummies".

"So, Gail. Do I anoint your head with oil, too?"

Gail laughed again. "I want to get into your world! Then I'll lend you my 'People' magazines and we'll be even."

"But—do you love me?"

Oh, I should have seen it coming—all of a sudden she began singing a rousing chorus from "Fiddler on the Roof". The woman seemed to have no lack of energy! Why could she not simply stick to the subject at hand?

"I was in that show in high school, that's how I remember all the words. I was Tevye's wife." Gail danced around the room, her hair bouncing, her face glowing.

"But Gail—do you love me?"

"Of *course* I do, you idiot. What, I've been talking to a *wall?*" And here she kissed me so deeply that for the first time in our married life, with Amber off at school and Mother off playing bridge with church women somewhere across the causeway, we had—oh, my God, we had relations in the *daytime*, although I had to hurry in case any parishioners came to the door.

For the first time I fully understood about "lying down in green pastures" and "having my soul restored". The Biblical David only had sheep.

I had Gail.

I made sure she had a new dress to wear as we greeted people after the next Sunday's service. As the person subject to me, I had to show how much I was caring for her. I had to—

*   *   *

DIRECTOR: George. Excuse me, George—

GEORGE (LOOKING UP AND AND BLINKING): Yes?

DIRECTOR: George, are you aware that you've been talking for the past twenty minutes without stopping? There are others who want a turn.

GEORGE: Oh! But I was just getting started. (TO THE GROUP): I only need five more minutes, if you do not mind.

DIRECTOR: Group? Is that all right with you? (LOOKS AROUND.) All right. Continue.

GEORGE: Thank you. Where was I?

GROUP MEMBER: You were talking about sex.

GEORGE (LOFTILY): I do not believe I specifically mentioned that word. But I do need to let you know about Leland Frye, my—

GROUP MEMBERS (IN UNISON, RATHER SARCASTICALLY): -- choir director and organist!

GEORGE (STARTLED): Oh! You *have* been paying attention! I am so used to watching people nod off when I begin my sermons—

GROUP MEMBER: We *have* noticed how much you enjoy controlling with words.

GEORGE: I most certainly do not!

GROUP MEMBER: What happens when you stop talking, George? Do you just (MAKES A ROUNDED GESTURE) "poof" away into nothing?

GEORGE: Well, I most definitely have something to say about *that*!

MEMBERS (NODDING): You sure do.

DIRECTOR: George. Is this how you want to spend your remaining five minutes?

GEORGE: Oh. No, of course not. Now, about Leland Frye . . . .

She was once Tevye's wife onstage, you know

"I have heard the mermaids singing, each to each.

I do not think that they will sing to me."

T.S. Eliot: The Love Song of J. Alfred Prufrock

Gail just couldn't believe her luck. Found the church in the phone book, called and found out when choir rehearsal was, made it look as though she was just happening by, and when she sang—damn, her voice was still there! The choir members seemed genuinely glad to have her singing with them, and even that fat old piano player had an almost-smile on her disapproving face.

"We could give Gail the soprano solo for three Sundays from now," said Mrs. Hitchcock. Since Mrs. Hitchcock was the only other soprano there, Gail knew this to be a sacrificial act of utter generosity. "Go ahead and try it, dear."

So here was a dilemma: Gail had only planned to drop in, find Father George, ask him out on a date, get ready to be rejected, and then go to the Banana Bay Inn and have a drink with her buddies. It wasn't supposed to be a *commitment*! But seven pairs of eyes were fixed upon her and she stammered, "Maybe I should sing it for you first. Then decide."

She was handed an anthem. It was an old one and she remembered with a jolt, a bit of it from her high school days. "I didn't know we did *church* music back then!" she thought.

(She also couldn't know that George would later make it one of his tasks to teach her the difference between sacred and secular music. "I get it, George, *I get it!* Sacred is stuffy and secular is fun!")

She was planning to make a mess of the song so she wouldn't be asked again, but her high school teacher's strict choral training got the better of her and she sang the solo with only a couple of mistakes.

The room of musicians clapped. Gail, breathing deeply, looked around, beaming. Father George was nodding his approval. "We have an angel from heaven here!" said Mrs. Hitchcock. "You must join our little choir and sing. Are you an Episcopalian?"

Ah. So that was the correct word. "No, Ma'am. Actually, I went to a number of different churches. I'm *baptized*, though," Gail announced proudly. The room of singers nodded.

"She'll need a robe," said Miss Peabody.

"She can have Mrs. Gustafson's. I think they're the same size."

"Oh, I don't want to take someone else's—"

"She doesn't sing with us anymore, since she's been bedridden."

"This last month she kept removing it, anyway."

"During the church service!"

"And she didn't stop *there*! Her underwear had pictures of *cats* on it!" Miss—what?—Eliott, one of the two altos said. My goodness, this was a funny bunch of people!

"You must have had a lot of voice training, my dear."

"No, no, just what I learned through school and then on the road with the Gorillas—"

"Then you're a *natural*! My, my."

"I sang in 'Fiddler on the Roof' and 'Oklahoma' and even 'Porgy and Bess'—of course in my school it was an all-white version," Gail added eagerly.

Miss Peabody then, to everyone's surprise, broke into the opening measures of "Summertime" on the piano— without music!-- and Gail, stepping up to the side of the old upright, sang her way through it.

Singing—it felt like a good strong drink to Gail; and how long had it been since she been able to let loose like this? Her body, emotions and mind felt like one. Trembling, her smile wobbly, she sat.

Mr. Foster stood up. His chair scraped across the floor behind him. "Ole Man Ribbah—" he intoned in a Russian-deep bass. "He jess keeps rollin' along." It was becoming a party even if he had mistaken Jerome Kern for "Porgy". And *she* had done it!

Father George was grinning so widely she thought his cheeks might burst. "Beautiful, beautiful!" he clapped. So *this* was the way to his heart—through music! Well, she should have no trouble then. "Father, do you know 'So in Love' from 'Kiss Me Kate'?" she asked.

"Shakespeare!" he announced. " 'The Taming of the Shrew'! Mother had the tape recording!" , and with Miss Peabody working hard at the piano to recall her Cole Porter, Gail and George fumbled through the seductive love song, looking into each other's eyes and harmonizing.

Gail was surprised at how pleasing a voice the priest had. The applause at the end was tardy, as though no one wanted to break up something rather intimate. Agnes Bowman had noisily excused herself to get a drink of water in the kitchen. Both singers took a little bow, with Father George looking as though he yearned to continue. He took a deep breath.

"Mother has cake and tea waiting for us in the rectory," he announced, "if that is all right with you, Miss Peabody." He then led the group in a round of appreciative applause for their pianist and they almost saw a smile. More party! Gail *loved* parties.

Gail took note: look, Father, I'm working miracles in your church for you already!

Miss Peabody merely nodded, apparently wrung out from remembering all that Gershwin. He led them in a closing prayer—something for good weather and good voices and angels singing—and then walked the chattering procession next door, where Gail had no idea that a redoubtable Mother was waiting.

If an entire church can adopt, the parishioners of St. Swithun's would do that with Gail and Amber—oh, the protesting Amber! Were all fourteen-year-olds this stubborn and sarcastic? Which one was the mother anyway, Gail or Amber? It seemed they took turns.

"You work at Penney's?" now asked Mrs. Dudley in the rectory kitchen. "And what do you do there?"

"Well, actually, that's where your son and I met," Gail stopped mumbling as the inside of her mouth exploded with flavor. She'd never tasted cake this good! "Excuse me, Mrs. Dudley—did you make this cake? I've never tasted anything so terrific!"

Gail winked at George (he was now "George" to her, as far as her conquest was concerned), who was grinning rather foolishly, observing the two women together. The older woman smiled. "I could show you how I do it," she said. "*Lots* of butter." They laughed, their heads close together.

"Ok," Gail thought—"this woman is the one to make friends with if I'm to get George." Her eyes met his and once more she was struck weak by the color. She studied his mother—eyes not the same at all. He must have inherited those heavenly eyes from his dad.

Where *was* his father, anyway? "I hope I meet Mr. Dudley also," she murmured. "Is he here with you in Banana Bay?"

"He's in the ground in Connecticut," was the terse reply from (all right, she knew now) the widow Dudley. Something wrong there, but Gail wasn't going to drop the level of polite conversation to probe. Probably not interesting, anyway.

"I sure hope you like Banana Bay. I've lived here under a year myself." (Better not explain about following a boyfriend here—like *that* worked out!) The women's conversation then turned to music and weather, gardening—Gail was not big on this and Mrs. Dudley was, and would she ever get used to this state of Florida that didn't have *lilacs?*—and bridge.

"Do you play bridge, Gail?"

"Nope. Never have."

"I never did until I came here. I'm in with a nice group of ladies. They take pity on me, a beginner, although they *have* warned me that I have a gambler's brain."

She laughed and so did Gail. "Don't tell my son. That would get him praying over me. My husband and I played a *lot* of poker, before George was born, way back."

Wow, she's all right! thought Gail, and they talked about the Florida heat driving them crazy. "You have to be careful outside—it can fry your brain!" The older woman nodded agreement. "And wow--I don't know how your son can wear all that black in this weather!"

Things took a different turn when Gail showed up at church with the rebellious Amber the next Sunday. "You want me to get you that cell phone? Then behave yourself!" Gail muttered.

"Oo-oh, you're trying to make a good impres-sion!" whined Amber.

"Want that cell phone? Then grow up a little and remember your manners."

Mrs. Dudley was appalled to learn at the coffee hour after church that Amber had to be in their apartment alone after the youngster came home from school. "That's just not *right*, now, is it, George?"

"Hm-m-m?"

"George, do listen. This child is parentless for several hours after school—"

"—it all depends on my hours at Penney's, Mrs. Dudley—"

"Well, it's just not right!"

And that is how Father George found himself the person who waited for Amber at her school every day and brought her home to the rectory, the teenager to encounter Mother's (to George, well-remembered) food inquisition:

"Did you eat lunch today at school?"

"Yes, Ma'am."

"What did you have?"

"Uh—I traded. Corn chips, cookies, a little Debbie, some Gatorade—"

"Good heavens! Your brain will absolutely turn to mush on that diet. Here—milk and a toasted cheese sandwich. Bacon and tomato on it ok? Good. Some carrot sticks, before you do your homework. *Uh uh uh*—better go wash your hands first. You don't know where they've been."

"I know where my hands have been."

"Well, then, you don't know where anyone *else's* hands have been, young lady."

Surprisingly for Gail, the oddly-matched duo turned out to have a mutual respect for each other, and Amber was given the run of the house, which was more than Gail had until after the wedding.

Having discovered all she could in the house (too many things had locks on them), Amber decided to investigate the church and then after startling Mrs.

Hitchcock, who was polishing the altar rail, wandered to the parish hall and inside it to the church office, where she found Father George alone and staring fixedly at a computer screen.

"What's up, George?" she asked, flinging herself into a chair and shoving her sneakered feet against the side of his desk

"Uh—oh, hello, Amber. I did not hear you come in."

"So—what's up?"

"I cannot get this blasted computer to do what I want it to do, and Mrs. Hitchcock has the afternoon off." He went back to staring at the screen, as though it would obey him.

"She's cleaning. And *I* know computers."

"Nonsense." He glowered at the skinny young girl who did not look a *thing* like Gail, about whom he had been daydreaming until he had just been interrupted.

"I *do*, though. Yours is an easy one. Easy-peasey."

"Do not joke with me, please, young lady."

Amber was offended. "I *never* joke and I've been learning computers since I was in pre-school. Want to see?"

The girl hoisted herself in front of the computer, pushing the priest out of the way. "George. Look what you did—you got it stuck on Firefox. Is that what you want?"

"I do not even know what that is." George watched in horror as Amber pushed a button and the screen went black. "What have you *done?*" he screeched. "My *sermon* is in that computer!"

"We're just starting over. Look." She pushed a button and the screen blossomed again. "You weren't cursing just now, were you, George?"

"*Father* George," the priest replied, but his attention was now on the screen. There was his sermon, appearing like magic! "How did you *do* that?"

"Don't they have computers in *Connecticut*, George?" Now this insufferable sarcastic child had pushed something else and a card game appeared.

"No, no, no *cards*! Get my sermon back!"

Thus began George's first computer lesson. He took notes which she dictated, and which, after Amber had gone home with a tired-looking Gail, he studied. But it was no use. Every time the youngster appeared at his door he had to invite her in and learn all over again.

What Amber enjoyed most was spending time with Mrs. Hitchcock's grandson's freckle-faced Matthew while he tinkered with Mrs. Dudley's Corolla in the driveway of the blue rectory.

"What more can you *do* to that thing, anyway? Add another couple of wheels"

"You just don't get it, do you, little girl? A car's gotta run perfectly or what's the use?"

"Hey. How old are you, Matt?"

"None of your business. I know *you're* fourteen. Just a squirt. My Grandma told me."

Amber's cheeks stung. "C'mon, really. Tell me. Or-- I'll tell her you had sex with me."

"You little brat! Better not talk like that—they'd put me in prison and you in a foster home. You crazy?" Her eyes filled with tears at his tone and she put her head down. "Okay, stop! I'm eighteen. And you shouldn't be talking that way. What'da you know about sex, anyway?"

"I know who I'm in *love* with, wise guy."

"Better not be me."

"Are you kidding?" Amber paused and watched for his reaction. "Don't you think *Lee* is cute?"

Matt hooted. "*Leland Frye*! You in love with *him*?" He snorted his soft drink through his nose in laughter.

"I don't see what's so funny." Really, for an older guy Matt acted like *such* a juvenile.

Matt wiped his face with the clean edge of an oily rag. "He's *gay*, infant. He is so definitely gay."

"He is *not!*"

"Yeah? He even tried hittin' on me once. Gay as grass. Just ask his boyfriend Emilio."

"*Emilio?* That kid with black hair who works at your grandmother's apartment building?"

"You got it. And Emilio's not a kid—he's 27. Why, you figure on turning *Lee* into a straight guy? You wanna *really* be in trouble?"

"You're lying to me, you—*idiot!*"

"*I'm* an idiot? Boy, if you're this dumb about *men* you'd probably kiss a *cow* and call it a bull."

"Yeah, well—at least *I* don't do *drugs!*"

She ducked as Matt threw his rag at her. "You little snitch! Shut up about that or I tell everybody at your school about you and *Lee!*"

George's mother, looking out the window, saw only how well the two teenagers were getting along.

Doris Dudley began inviting Gail and Amber more and more often to stay for dinner. At first it seemed to Gail to be out of politeness, but then she sensed some conflicting emotions from ("and that's what she's gonna be—my mother-in-law!") Mrs. Dudley.

Not my choice, was what Gail sensed from George's mother. *You are not my choice for my only son, my pride, my joy, the one I have Groomed For God.*

Gail wasn't sure if she herself was in love with George or with the thrill of the hunt. But at least she had something she could give George that his mother could not.

And one night when she showed him her apartment while Amber and DeeDee were at a movie, she did. George, gasping, raised himself from her sweaty sheets. "I've—I've never done anything like that before!" he panted.

"You were so good at it," Gail lied.

"You—Gail! You need to *marry* me!"

"Why, George!"

"Gail—I love you or I never would have taken advantage of you in this way. And I am a *priest*! Oh, I did not mean for that to happen! What will you think of me?"

He sank down again on her bed. "When is your roommate coming home with Amber?"

"Should be another half hour. Maybe more—they like to stop for pizza."

"Did I give them enough money for pizza?"

"George, honey, you gave them enough for a steak dinner!"

"Then—could we try this again? And a little-- slower this time?"

They were married the next month, in October. A month without sex. George's sense of order had returned—"I shall want you more when we are legally and in the eyes of the church, married." Doris Dudley, eyeing her preoccupied son, knew just what had happened.

Their marriage counseling was overseen by the priest at St. Barnabus' church. Both Gail and George thought him a "ponderous windbag" and giggled about it after their sessions.

Gail could see that George enjoyed sharing private laughter with her. "I'll make him a good wife," she thought. "The sex will get better. Amber will have a father. I can quit work. Oh, what'll I wear for the wedding? Will it be ok with George if I wear white? How far off the shoulder can I go? How can I get DeeDee to not show up with her bar bums? How will the church feel about me? And *how* can I keep Gladys Hitchcock from singing "O Promise Me" at our wedding, when she's rehearsing it now at every choir practice?"

She had no idea George's thoughts had only one theme and even he did not know whether he was praying or swearing: "My God! What have I done? What am I doing? *What am I doing? How many days until I have sex again?*"

The second prayer/swear: "How can I get Miss Peabody to use a little less volume on the organ when Mrs. Hitchcock sings her solo?"

When he and Mother had arrived in Banana Bay last August and had been shown around, he had attempted to remove his sunglasses, but the glare stabbed through him. Mr. Campbell, observing this, had said, "Be careful in this Florida sun, Father George. It can drive a man crazy. It's not like up north, you know." And all of a sudden here he *was*—crazy in love with Gail! It took all of his effort to pay attention at the budget meeting. He was certain he could smell her on his skin.

That same Mr. Campbell was eyeing him now. Was he reading his rector's mind? George felt his face redden.

I had better get married as soon as possible, thought George guiltily. The flesh was so *weak*, when it was near Gail's--!

Saint Paul had written, "Better to marry than to burn in hell." That was because he was certain Christ was returning at any moment. "Please, God, don't send Your Son back just yet," George now prayed. "Not until I get a chance to enjoy more—time-- with Gail!"

Every sermon for the next three weeks had something to do with love. George did not notice his theme until he observed some teenagers in the congregation snickering and Agnes Brown pouting.

The next Sunday he concentrated on the labors of Job.

V. In which George Endures his New Organist

"I was angry with my friend; / I told my wrath, my wrath did end.

I was angry with my foe; / I told it not, my wrath did grow.

And I watered it in fears / Night and morning with my tears,

And I sun-ned it with smiles/ And with soft deceitful wiles.

And it grew both day and night/ Till it bore an apple bright,

And my foe beheld it shine, /And he knew that it was mine.

And into my garden stole/ When the night had veiled the pole;

In the morning, glad I see / My foe outstretched beneath the tree."

William Blake: A Poison Tree

I have already discussed how the large and unfortunate Miss Peabody tripped over a more-unfortunate cat, which retired that perennial organist and forced us to look for another one. I can tell you from experience that good ones are almost impossible to find, especially here in Banana Bay.

And then along came Mr. Leland Frye, Boy Wonder of the Keyboard and the parish fell in love with him. You will recall how against his being hired I was. Something about him--.

Of course he had to try out for the post first, so he played on the last Sunday before Advent, the last Sunday in November this year, after we had been without a regular organist for about a month. It was Christ the King Sunday, a festive affair before the somber four Sundays of Advent take over, and then the twelve days of Christmas, at breakneck speed, occur.

With proper Episcopalians the Christmas season does not last just one day, December 25, but twelve days more, up until Epiphany—not that people wait that long to take down their Christmas trees. Nor do we sing and play Christmas carols during Advent. Advent, the four weeks before Christmas, is a time of solemn preparation!

Yet tell that to the parishioners hurtling themselves to the Banana Bay Yacht Club all through December for drinks and good cheer, with never a brunch invitation to me.

Christmas this year was to be a terrible letdown, without snow and ice and darkness before dinnertime. And how does one *possibly* with good cheer and true Christmas spirit purchase a Christmas tree, in the midst of having to turn on the air conditioner in the car on the way to the tree sale run by the Boy Scouts in the mall parking lot!

I had only the month of December (oh yes, he had been hired, four yeas to my nay) to train Mr. Leland Frye in the proper chants and music for these very special seasons in the Church. "Mr. Frye, I think it will help you to take notes—"

"I've trained myself to have a very good memory, Father George."

"As you will. Now. We have four weeks of Advent, beginning next Sunday. The third Sunday is Rose Sunday. There will also be caroling, although *why* that is allowed to happen before Christmas is beyond me. Another of this church's traditions which I have inherited."

"Got it. Rose. Caroling."

"There will be a Sunday of Lessons and Carols, as practiced in England. Began in Coventry, as I recall."

"Coventry. Got it."

"In addition," I continued, piqued by his self-confident attitude and still fuming over the fact that he had been the only viable candidate for the job, "there will be a children's program on Christmas Eve afternoon and then the Midnight Mass, with an extra anthem."

"I've been thinking about that," said Mr. Frye cautiously, "How about for Christmas we try a solo instead of the extra anthem? It would relieve the choir some and your wife does have a beautiful voice. Oh, I can just *hear* her singing 'O Holy Night'. Like a choir of angels."

Ah! Right out of gate he was offering me a dilemma: if I said "Yes", then he would be getting his way. If I said "No", then I would be forbidding Gail to use one of her talents—her voice. There was only one answer: "I shall give the matter some prayerful consideration."

"Do, please. Choirs tend to get such a *strained* sound at this time of year."

What an upstart thing to say!

"The ones I've been in, anyway. The way they go out looking for any other Christian church that is singing 'The Messiah' during December, in addition to all the music they have to practice here at St. Swithun's!"

I had to give it to him: he rebounded well. Very well indeed.

"And is there a Christmas morning service, Father George?"

"There is indeed. It *is* the birthday of our Lord, you know." He did not respond. "Just the organ, though, and carols sung by the parishioners. Many people come to that service."

"Have you ever wondered if perhaps it's because the choir is *not* singing?"

"Certainly not! Many of them just do not like to drive at night." Good grief, was the man going to argue with me over every jot and tittle?

"Now, Mr. Frye—"

"Please call me Leland. Or better, call me Lee."

"You are fortunate, because this year Christmas Eve falls on a Saturday, so that means—"

"—I won't have to play for a Sunday service and then a Christmas Eve service that night, if Christmas falls on a Monday. I've had to do that in the past—*exhausting*."

I looked at him skeptically. "You must have been about 15, to play then." I glanced at his fingers, long and slim—quite a contrast to Miss Peabody's, which were so pudgy that it seemed a miracle that she was able to fit them on just one key at a time.

"I was young, but I was ready for *anything*. I am now, too."

He smiled down at me. Did *everyone* in his generation have perfect teeth?

"Anything else, Father George? My day job won't get in the way, will it? I just can't survive on only an organist's pay, alas. Thank goodness for my employment at your Mr. Campbell's plant nursery—so charitable of him to see my plight. Your begonias could use a little less water, by the way. We don't want root rot now, do we?" I waited to see if he was going to ask for a bigger salary, but then he said, "Ah, the arts, the arts—so necessary to life and so underpaid. Like *your* calling, I'm sure."

"*My* calling is not up for discussion."

Mr. Frye retreated slightly. "Oh, no, oh, of course not. Please don't misinterpret—"

"Just--be sure to hand me copies of all the music you select, for me to approve."

"I wouldn't have it any other way. Rumor has it that you're quite the musician yourself."

*   *   *

I did not correct him, but that was unhappily not totally true: when I was in junior high school our church youth group went roller skating. I almost did not go, because I had never skated and was afraid of falling and making a fool of myself. Only the idea that the lanky Sandra Barber would be there kept me from staying home. I fantasized about skating around the rink, resplendent with magical lights, with me arm in arm, hand in hand with Sandra, gazing up into her freckled face.

None of that happened and it did not matter, because when we got there I became totally fascinated by the organist at the Wurlitzer organ. Oh, the *music* she made! It was glorious, thrilling! I spent the entire afternoon clutching the rail and watching her.

When I came home I told Mother, "It is my desire to take organ lessons, please."

"No way, Ho-zay," my father said. He was sprawled across the sofa. He had a beer in his hand and a sports program on TV. Mother muted the TV and he protested, loudly.

"Here," she said, throwing the remote control at his stomach. The two of us retreated to the kitchen. "So how was the skating rink?" she asked as she poured me a glass of milk.

"Oh, Mother! Honestly, I want to take some organ lessons. Do you think Dr. Evans at church would give me some?"

I did not ask quietly enough. From the living room came, "I said *no lessons* and it's *gonna* be *no lessons*! I don't want any more of a fruitcake for a son than I already *got!*" His words hurt so badly that I had a hard time swallowing.

"I'll look into it tomorrow," said Mother to me, frowning toward the living room. When she left to argue with him, I poured a little of his Wild Turkey from the cupboard into my milk, to settle my nerves and my feeling of rejection by Sandra. The glass was empty and rinsed out at the sink before she returned with money for my first lesson.

And that is how I went through a year of learning. So if Mr. Leland Frye, M.A. thinks he is the only one around here who is proficient at the electronic keyboard, he has another think coming!

"By the way, Father George—I've found myself a *very* charming apartment in the same building where your mother lives. She's teaching me how to play bridge. I think she's just *entrancing!* Such a dear. And I hope it's all right with you that I'm giving Amber some free piano and organ lessons. I think there's a real music gene thing-y going on there. Ta-ta."

So. It was turning out that he was not satisfied merely with wanting to enchant my wife with Christmas solos as bait; he had to lure my new stepdaughter away from me, too. And now *Mother*--!

Gail sang "O Holy Night" at Christmas. It was beautiful, uplifting. You could tell she had had extra private rehearsals with Mr. Frye (I still refused to call him by his first name!). Her voice went up, up, up into the rafters of St. Swithun's and mine were not the only eyes that were wet. Even Mother's eyes were glistening.

Mother! I half-seriously considered performing an exorcism for her, she had changed so since we had moved here! Allow me to enumerate what had happened to her in just five months:

1. she learned to drive a car;

2. she took up exercising and losing weight;

3. she stopped cooking my favorite meals and giving me fresh sheets every day;

4. she learned to play bridge;

5. she moved out of the rectory right after Gail and I married, and into her own apartment. And

6. the worst! The *worst!* I repeat our telephone conversation *verbatim*:

"George, I know you want to have lunch with me, but I'm very busy today, Dearie."

(I breathed a massive sigh. "Dearie" was something that Mr. Leland Frye was fond of saying, and now my own mother--! She had never called me "Dearie" in my entire life until now.)

"Oh? And what are your immoveable plans, that you cannot spend some quality time with your son?"

"Now don't be that way, George. My bridge club is having a tournament at the Yacht Club, and—"

"The Yacht Club?"

"Why, yes."

"The Banana Bay Yacht Club and Golf Course? *That* Yacht Club?"

"Why—yes, George."

"I suppose you will be having *brunch*."

"Well, I guess so. That's what we had last time."

"*Last time?*" I could feel my face burning. "There was a *last time?*"

"Oh, George, it's not a big deal. It's not as though we *won*." I snorted, like a horse. "I really have to scoot, Dearie. Bye." There was a pause. "George? You still there?"

"Yes, Mother."

"Look, why don't you come over for dinner tomorrow evening, just you and I? Let Gail and Amber find something on their own. It'll just be the two of us, like old times. Wouldn't you like that, George? I'll make meat loaf your special way, without onions. And George, you haven't seen the place since I decorated. Lee and Emilio helped me choose the colors. I never would have thought to choose these particular shades myself, but both those boys have such an eye for—"

I had by now in my leather chair slumped almost to the floor. Lord, I prayed, I am under attack. From without and within. And Emilio? Who the—heck was Emilio? And why was my own mother in cahoots with Leland Frye? Was *everyone* around me going mad?

Could it be Florida? People wearing shorts in December? The rather lackadaisical attitude toward Advent? I knew the color pink was used in police stations to calm convicts. Perhaps the color blue had the opposite effect and Mother's brain was going haywire as a result.

Ten a.m. be damned. I needed, and took, a drink from my private cache. It could have been more than one. Probably more, since I was under attack. And I was alone.

Ah, I thought, fondling my glass and watching the oily amber coat the—amber, that is funny, wonder if she named her daughter for the color of liquor. Where was I? Ah, yes--who can recall his or her first drink? It is said that if you can, and in much detail, like recalling your first kiss or the first time you got—you know—all right, *laid!--*, it means you are an alcoholic.

I well remember the first time I got laid. Only four months ago. And I'm still not good at it, for Gail anyway. *I* sleep fine afterward. That is one advantage of having Mother in her own place and out of earshot. Might Gail, in her frustration, be seeing old Lee on the side? Would she? That *kid*? Did she think I was an old man? What did I know about her comings and goings, anyway? Working in the thrift shop, indeed, at the very hour I had Bible class and could not drop over to see if she was really there.

Earshot. All right—raise my glass to a shot for the left ear. And then one for the right ear. It is my day off, anyway. Monday. First Gail had to work (Why is she insisting on continuing to work? "I like the excitement, George." The excitement of *Penney's?*) This is old Lee's day off, too. Maybe I should just wander over to Penney's and see if she is actually—(now what do I need to buy, that I can tell her?), and then Mother's—no, I cannot go to Mother's; she is off to her glorious yacht club, Banana Bay's Heaven On Earth. She will probably have a good bottle of wine with her *brunch*.

Wine. I can still remember my first taste of sacramental wine. Such a little taste it was, a wafer dipped into a chalice and placed upon my young tongue. I wanted more!

"Young tongue"—that's funny. Maybe it will go into my next sermon.

* * *

DIRECTOR: George. George.

GEORGE: Yes?

DIRECTOR: Your five minutes is up. It's someone else's turn.

GROUP MEMBER (MALE): George thinks he's more fascinatin' than the rest of us, just 'cause he's a priest.

GEORGE (PRIMLY): I shall take that under advisement.

GROUP (FEMALE): George, will you let someone else have a turn?

GEORGE: Well, certainly. Far be it from me to be accused of—

GROUP MEMBERS (TOGETHER): George! *SHUT UP!*

GEORGE (RISING): I am leaving. I do not have to stay here, do I?

DIRECTOR: There's the door. But if you leave you will have accomplished nothing. You'll go back to the same situation you left. And remember—you're walking out on us. We're not abandoning *you*.

GEORGE (HEATEDLY): *They* made me leave! My own church!

GROUP MEMBER: All of us were made to leave, George.

GEORGE: What do you mean, "*all*"?

DIRECTOR: Everyone in this group is a priest, George. Even me. I'm a recovering alcoholic.

GEORGE (SHOCKED): And you dare call yourself our *leader*?

DIRECTOR (UNFAZED): You called yourself a leader at St. Swithun's.

GEORGE: I—I need a drink. All right? I am admitting that I could use a drink right now.

DIRECTOR: Guys, let's take a break. Coffee, iced tea out on the front porch.

GROUP MEMBER: How come there's always only decaf?

DIRECTOR (WITH A SMILE): You really want to put high-test into George?

GEORGE (DESPERATELY): I do not even need to *be* here! Wherever the hell *here* is! Nobody has told me! Nobody has called me, nobody has come to get me out of here--!

GROUP MEMBER (FEMALE): Hey, guys—I vote that after our break we let George finish his story. What do you say?

FIRST GROUP MEMBER (MALE): Shit, might as well. He's just about ready to crack.

GEORGE: Crack? I do not *crack*! (LOOKING AROUND) But thank you. You are all most kind.

SECOND GROUP MEMBER (MALE): George, I'll know you've cracked when you start using contractions!

GEORGE: Not I. I do not believe in them. A lazy way to talk.

THIRD GROUP MEMBER (MALE): "I believe in God the Father, God the Son and God the Holy Contractions".

GEORGE: That is just plain scandalous.

FIRST GROUP MEMBER: "Holy Contractions"! Sounds like Batman and Robin, out to save the world.

GROUP MEMBER (FEMALE): Like our George here. Tough job, George, holding it all together.

GROUP MEMBER: Yeah, how do you do it, George? Decide what's right and then get everyone to follow you and your beliefs?

SECOND GROUP MEMBER: Even Jesus couldn't accomplish that.

GROUP MEMBER (MALE): Maybe George can show Jesus how to do it—save the world.

GEORGE (QUOTING RIGHTEOUSLY): "All falls apart; The centre cannot hold—" T.S. Eliot. *Not* a contraction!

GROUP MEMBER (FEMALE): Uh, actually, George, it's "Things fall apart; the centre cannot hold;" and it's W.B. Yeats, not T.S. Eliot.

GEORGE (TAKEN ABACK, BUT RALLYING IMMEDIATELY): And I maintain that *I* am right and *you* are wrong, until proven otherwise. Anyone have a book of poetry here? Thought not.

SECOND GROUP MEMBER (LIGHTLY): My God, Alberta—were we like that when we first come here and dumped on you? I weep for you and I applaud your therapeutic ways. (HANDS IN A PRAYING CONFIGURATION, TOWARD THE DIRECTOR.)

DIRECTOR: C'mon, gang. Let's break. Fifteen minutes. If you insist on smoking, and you know who you are, (GENERAL LAUGHTER) please use the ashtrays that are outside.

GEORGE: But I am not even supposed to be here! My church did this to me--! And no one has told me where I am, except when I look outside I see that I am in the wilds of Florida, without another house in sight, let alone a road!

DIRECTOR: Give us all a break now, George. Fifteen minutes. Walk around if you want. We've got some lovely scenery here.

GEORGE (SARCASTICALLY): What? Scrub palm? Sand?

GROUP MEMBER: Rattles-s-s-snakes. Coral s-s-snakes. Pygmy rattlers, worse than the big ones. Not to mention cottonmouths .And if you fall in the lake, which is probably full of gators, then *I* get dibs on being next to talk! (GENERAL LAUGHTER.)

* * *

However these relentless Hounds of Hell pester me, I shall not reveal to them my shameless night of phoning in to a radio talk show—primarily because I do not remember most of it. They have no way of knowing that I have already poured out my soul, while lubricated, to a disc jockey and his merciless sidekick. Apparently upon falling, there is no bottom to which I am able to plunge. And why not? I am G.O.D.

VI. Whereupon George's Soul is a-thirst for God and the Rest of him for Something Else to Drink

> "Down, down into the darkness of the grave
> Gently they go, the beautiful, the tender, the kind;
> Quietly they go, the intelligent, the witty, the brave.
> I know. But I do not approve. And I am not resigned."
>
> Edna St. Vincent Millay: Dirge Without Music

February 14—I remember this date well because I have a dozen red roses wrapped in beautiful green tissue paper in the car and I am going to surprise Gail with them. I never knew they would be so *expensive* on this one day. Perhaps, I think, I will give her a half-dozen and the other half to Mother—yes, that seems like a good plan to me.

I stop for a red light at the intersection of U.S. #1 and the Causeway Road, the one that goes east to the 1/2 mile wide sand spit of land which snakes down between the Indian River and the Atlantic Ocean. The high-rise bridge is ahead of me and I am on my way to pay a call on one of the few members of St. Swithun's who lives this far away from the western edge of Banana Bay Mainland and my church.

Banana Bay Beach--*that* is where the Banana Bay Yacht Club has its existence. I am troubling myself with the idea that Mother has seen more activity inside that club than I have, when a red convertible sports car (with two? three?) figures in it comes hurtling toward me from the east, careens through the red light, leaps across the intersection, and lands upside down not thirty feet behind me.

There is an immediate flashing blue light in my rearview mirror—apparently an officer of the law is a few cars in back of me—what good fortune! A jumble of people now have pulled over and alighted from their cars. All either have cell phones to their ears, or are taking photos. I start to join them.

"Sir," a young policeman showing up suddenly at my car window says to me, "I must ask you to stay in your car." He then walks over to the other drivers, gesturing to them to move out of the way. They, somewhat reluctantly it seems to me, obey him.

I leave my vehicle, first making sure I have locked it behind me. The policeman is again at my side.

"Sir," he repeats, "I must ask you to stay in your car."

"But," I protest, "I can be of help."

"Sir," he repeats, "please remain in your car. I need you not to be in the way when the ambulance gets here."

As if I would be in the way! I bristle. "Officer, I am an Episcopal priest and I need to be of help."

He now looks more carefully at me. Behind us there is pandemonium. Some very muscled young men have managed to upright the sports car and I can see that there are two—no, I was right, three-- people lying in the street in quite crumpled positions.

"The best thing you can do to help, Father, is to stay in your car."

"But I—I *need* to help!"

"Sir. Stay in your car."

This all sounds now so calm, but in fact he is trying to talk to me and others, and also to motion traffic around the site of the accident. I hear the wail of the ambulance in the distance. Another blue-light patrol car has joined the scene. Pandemonium! I head toward the sports car.

"Sir! You must listen to me!"

"You do not appear to understand—"

"No, Father, *you* don't understand. I'm trying to keep you out of harm's way. There's a possibility of gas igniting. Tell you what—I'll call you as soon as we need you. Now please pull your car out of the lane of traffic. I promise I'll call you if you're needed."

"But—!" Why does he not understand that I have trained myself all my life to be of help? Does this collar mean *nothing*?

I read in frustration the officer's badge—Robbins. Well, I can remember *that,* in case I have to report him: Robbins, blue like a blue robin, like the church. Does he not recognize who I *am*?

He watches while I unlock my car door and climb inside; then he turns to go back to the accident. I am, I find, shaking—from the accident or from the altercation with Officer Robbins' obstinacy? I open the glove compartment and happily there is still a small container of Scotch there. Just so--I need a drink or two to calm my nerves. It is not every day one witnesses an accident! And then is spoken to in such a dismissive manner!

I have replaced the empty container by the time Officer Robbins knocks on my window. I am now not in a rescuing frame of mind. Let him get someone else. I roll down my window.

"Father, you can help now." His tone is somber and I suspect, apologetic. "There's a man who won't make it. The other two are so full of drugs that they landed kind of soft. They should be all right."

Oh, so *now* he wants to be my friend. All right. I follow him to a man on a stretcher. A woman in a bloodied white outfit bending over him looks up at us and shakes her head—we are too late. "Sorry, Father," she says.

I make the sign of the Cross over the victim. That is all I can do. I certainly shall report Officer Robbins for not allowing me to help.

Then I take a closer look at the man on the stretcher.

It cannot be, but *is*: Gladys Hitchcock's grandson Matthew, the one who showed Mother how to drive, who found the Toyota for her. There is red all over the ground underneath him, red like the roses I bought for Gail and Mother. How is there so much red, now turning darker into black, black like my suit, black turning to-- white? There is a roaring in my head. I stumble unseeing onto the boy's right leg. His eyes, oh, his eyes like a dead bird's . . .

"Watch him," the woman warns. "He's gonna faint."

And now my knees give out and I catch myself from falling directly onto the teenager.

No, I do not catch myself; Officer Robbins has grasped me with a large arm. "Shock," he is saying to the woman. "Father, you need to sit down. You need someone to drive you home. Father—excuse me, Father, but have you been drinking?"

"Of course not! It is just—I know this boy. I know this boy. I know this boy—"

Oh Lord help me I knew this boy.

* * *

Matthew's death presents me with my third funeral at St. Swithun's—my second, if you do not count Cat-Mandoo.

There is a magnificent solemnity to those opening words, " 'I am Resurrection and I am Life,' says the Lord", which I intone as I march up the aisle, circling around the small cloth-draped box holding the ashes of Gladys Hitchcock's grandson. Mrs. Hitchcock chose the cloth from others in the altar guild room, since it was one that she herself had embroidered some years before, never dreaming that . . . .

The choir is supposed to sing, but they choke so on their tears that I am the only one up front able to make my way through "Amazing Grace". (I had waited for Mr. Leland Frye to give me some backtalk about this hymn, but he, fortunately for him, did not. After my altercation with Officer Robbins I was ready for almost anything.)

Gail keeps blowing her nose. Tears are even running down Mr. Leland Frye's face as he plays and this aspect of him startles me. I catch sight of Amber. Her face is like mine, like stone.

I do not know quite what to say at the reception following the service, so I escape to the rectory while all the hugging and more tears are going on in the parish hall. Mother is standing with her arm around Gladys Hitchcock's waist. Matthew's mother (not a member of our church, to Mrs. Hitchcock's chagrin), looking very much like him with all her freckles (Oh, Lord, freckles like Sandra Barber's) which stand out today against her white face, crushes a paper napkin in her fist. She stands numb with grief while the voluble Agnes Brown natters on.

The rectory is so still I can hear the clock in my den ticking. I pour a drink to calm myself and settle into my leather chair.

The door opens. "George?" asks a small voice.

I look up. It is Amber. "George—," she starts and then flings herself at me, sobbing, almost spilling my Scotch. We sit this way for quite some time. When, spent, she falls asleep against my chest, I finish my drink. I would like a second one, even a third, but I do not dare move. I have never in my life been this close to a youngster and for such a long stretch of time. Something inside me begins to ache.

I do not have any idea what it is.

*   *   *

GROUP MEMBER (MALE): Weeping for yourself, George.

GEORGE: Ridiculous. I have nothing to weep for.

SECOND GROUP MEMBER (MALE): That was a beautiful thing you did, just being there for Amber.

GEORGE: I was not being there for her! She just happened to find me and she was sad.

DIRECTOR: She came looking for a father. For a Daddy. A-ah. That was a *big* sigh just then, George.

GEORGE: It's just that you all wear me out and confuse me!

GROUP MEMBER (MALE): He said "it's"! He used a contraction!

GEORGE: I most certainly did not!

(GROUP MEMBERS): Yes, you did! We heard you! Breakthrough! Breakthrough!

*   *   *

In short order then, to satisfy this group from Hades that I have been incarcerated with, out here in God-knows-where: the Saturday after Valentine's Day Gail disappeared.

Her roses were hardly wilted, even from having been in a closed car, and when Gail learned what had happened she insisted on putting them in the altar vases. "For

Matt's funeral," she cried. She cried for quite a long time and then she phoned Mother and she cried some more. When Mrs. Hitchcock and her daughter came to the rectory to plan the music for the service Gail hugged them in a way I would not have been able to do. I was proud of her then, to be my wife.

The funeral was on Friday. She was gone, vanished, the very next day. *Just like that!*

Oh, she left me a note. "I have to get away and think. Back soon. Love, Gail"—with a small circle and a tiny smile inside its circumference. No details at all—where did she go? Think about *what?*

To further consternate me, on Sunday there was no Mr. Leland Frye, either! "He phoned me," said Mother. (Mother, of all people!) "He said he had the flu and wouldn't be there for the service."

"But—how did he sound?"

"What do you mean, George? He just sounded like Lee."

"He could have given some warning. This is most galling to me."

"Well, say hello to Gail for me. And Amber."

"Oh. Yes. I most certainly will. Uh—they are not with you, are they?"

"Why, no. What a question."

"Yes, well—I think I hear someone at the door. Good-bye, Mother."

So. This was a fine state of affairs—first Gail gone and then Mr. Frye. Gail *and* Mr. Frye!

A faint thrumming worked its way behind my forehead. Could it be possible--?

But first I had a service to get through. I had not slept much the night before, worrying about Gail. Also, I had become used to having her in my bed and so it was a long night. I could not even remember what the topic of my sermon was.

To my astonishment Amber was standing in front of the church when I got there. "What are you—? I expected you to be away with your mother!" I gasped. Amber appeared quite calm.

"George, you look terrible."

"*Where did you spend the night, young lady?*"

"In my bedroom. Didn't you hear me? Boy, you must have been three sheets--."

"Excuse me! I need to know where your mother is!"

"She's done this before. She always comes back, George."

"*Father* George," a tall man corrected her as he passed us on the church steps.

"Wow. That was a real cowboy," Amber mused. I pulled her aside rather roughly. "Ow!"

"Amber—where does she go?"

"But did you see that guy--?"

"Amber!"

"Oh. Mom. She never tells me where she goes. But, George, I told you—she always comes back." The church bell tolled at that moment—Mr. Campbell faithfully doing his job.

"I don't have an organist!" I hissed at her. "Leland is sick!-- so he *says*!"

She gaped. "Lee is sick?"

"Yes, and my hunch is that—," (Could I say this to a child? But I rushed on) "—my strong hunch is that they've gone off together!"

Amber wrinkled her young brow. "But why?"

"Obvious reasons! Well, perhaps not to a *child!* They are in love with each other!"

And to my irritation she stifled a laugh.

"Oh yes, laugh. But you will see what I have suspected for months--!"

Mr. Campbell appeared at the door. "Father George, we don't know what to do about the service. It's all higgledy-piggledy inside without you and Mrs. Dudley and Mr. Frye—. Good morning, Miss Amber." he added politely. She nodded to him.

"And now no music!" I groaned.

"George—I can play."

'Not now, Amber."

"I can play, George. Not great, but you and I can do the service together. Just give me a minute to turn on the organ."

And that fearless child pulled herself up to the old two manual Baldwin and opened the spiral-bound musician's hymnal to the opening hymn, which fortunately was number 680, "Oh God, our help in ages past" and in the key of C. She mostly played the melody line, and did not use the foot pedals at all, but between her and the choir, we made it through the service.

There was no offertory anthem, of course, under the circumstances, but Mr. Foster, our bass, volunteered to sing "Rock'd in the Cradle of the Deep" (An old hymn. Colonial days. Emma Hart Willard. Started first girls' high school in United States, Troy, New York. Still in existence. Friend of Lafayette: Mr. Foster explained all this, eager to educate the congregation; but all I could think of was Gail and where *was* she?). He was more than eager to sing it *a capella*, to applause, which was unheard of in my church.

They applauded even louder the flushed Amber at the conclusion of the closing hymn, which was number 533,

"How wondrous and great, Thy works, God of Praise", in the key of G and thankfully only two verses long.

"Mr. Frye taught me," she announced, beaming. "It's a little like using a computer." She was actually quite good-looking when she smiled, I discovered. Was she wearing *lipstick*?

My suspicions mounted. Had Old Lee—he no longer deserved to be called by his formal name!-- taught her those hymns, knowing he was going to be absent? That would be just like him, sneaky, devious, and using an innocent child to further his nefarious plans! In my mind he was turning into the villain on TV in the Dudley Do-Right cartoons.

I needed to rescue Gail from him! Where in the world could she be? It took all my courage not to panic. Of course I prayed: "Lord, bring her back unharmed and I swear I will be a better person." Although I was not sure how I could be.

To all those who asked, I responded that Gail was away visiting friends and that Mr. Frye had the flu. Mother invited Amber and me to dinner and we accepted, but I could hardly eat. What if the phone rang while I was out? What if she had had an accident and was calling out for me and I was sitting here in Mother's apartment, enjoying a meal while she was somewhere starving? What if she--?

"She has your cell phone number, George," said Mother, as though reading my mind. "Quit fidgeting. That won't bring her back any sooner."

"She might call the rectory," I answered in a rather grumpy voice.

"If Amber says she's done this before and she'll be back, then don't worry, George. My land, sometimes I wanted so badly to run away from your *father*—," but she stopped when I frowned at her. Mother insisted on having Amber stay with her for the night. That was an admirable plan as far as I was concerned, and Amber, oddly, did not argue. I came home to sit by the phone and have a drink or two to help me figure things out.

My fantasies about Gail and that arrogant Leland Frye increased as the night wore on. How dared he do that to her? And to abandon a husband, a man of the cloth!—and a child, and an entire congregation, just like that!

Well, I would not take *either* of them back. This was beyond the pale. How could I take Gail back, after she had spent time being—used—by Leland? How could I possibly kiss that mouth after it had spent the week end on Leland's? How could I touch that body which was possibly now in some cheap motel someplace, being touched by *him*? This was unbearable!

But I loved her! I needed to take her back, to forgive her her wrongdoing, to help her up from her knees begging my forgiveness, to be generous. Yes, generous even in my grief.

Well, Old Lee was out of a job, *that* was for certain! And if he thought I would give him a letter of recommendation—ha, just let him try!

Wait. Where did he live? They might not have gone out of town. Did Gail have any money of her own to do that? I searched for her purse in vain. Perhaps they were in Leland's love nest right now! I should surprise them—no, no, I did not want to see them like that. But I should! I needed to view for myself, to divest myself of her!

But she was my Gail, I moaned.

In the end I merely finished my bottle, then fell into a fitful sleep in my unmade bed, to awaken to the familiar blue glow from the sunlight and the church.

*   *   *

Here is the shameful part: I climbed into bed and turned on the radio that Sunday night, after I finished my bottle and fretted about Gail. It was set to a station she liked, although I would not let her listen to it while I was in the room. Outrageous Ollie (funny we had the same middle name) and a woman named Georgina—now was this a sign for me or not, my two names on the same program?—were transmitting a talk show, as they called it.

"HELLO!" laughed Outrageous Ollie in a hearty voice. He sounded as though he had more teeth in his mouth than the average person. "This is 'Confession Session' and you're on the air! What's your confession tonight? No need to use your name, just tell us whazzup? C'mon, give us a call. We-e-e're listening!"

I dialed the number he gave. Actually I had to dial it three times before I got it right, and to my surprise was put through to Outrageous himself.

"I have a mid-middle name just like yours," I told him.

"You *do*! Meathead, Horny Devil, Speed Freak?"

"Olive—Oliver."

"Hey, guys, here's *Oliver*! And what brings you to Confession Session, Ollie Number Two?"

Surprisingly, having my middle name abbreviated did not offend me, even though I heard a woman laugh. "I—I need to confess that I am not yet a fan of your state of Florida."

"Whoa, gang, we got us a gen –you-wine *Northerner* here and he's gonna tell us what's wrong with us! Go ahead, Ollie. What is it—the politics, the weather, the sugar barons?"

"No! It is that—people seem to *change* when they live here and have to learn to watch out for those big palmetto bugs and lizards underfoot and the trees are so different and there is no real dirt except what you buy at the store and the people— the people—they knock down buildings that are not even a hundred years old, like that old two-story one whose photo I saw and it was historical and somebody told me it was haunted and they replace them with pharmacies and gas stations!"

"Yeah?"

"And, Ollie—may I call you Oliver, Mr. Outrageous?-- the people here seem so—happy! Like they do not need me for anything. And what happens to the ghosts—do they have to haunt a *drugstore* now? And they do not seem to mind sweating and I find that offensive."

"I didn't know ghosts sweated." Oh, Outrageous Oliver is just not *getting it*!

"Mebbe while they're hauntin' the drugstore they steal some deodorant." There is a raucous laugh from someone—Georgina?

"It is more than that! It is that people here are like immigrants—they come from somewhere else and they are proud of that fact, but then they settle right in here and I have not been able to do that. Did I say that people sweat a lot here? Even in church?"

"Hell, that's no confession, Ollie."

"Even my mother. She *never* sweated in Connecticut. But now she does and she plays bridge at the Yacht Club and it is like a tree fort that I am not allowed to get in, but *she* can. Because people *like* her and they do not seem to respect my leadership and I cannot figure out why, Oliver!"

"Maybe you need to start wearin' some deodorant yourse'f, Ollie," chimes in a woman's voice.

"Hey, movin' on. Thanks for your confession, man."

"I'm just getting to it! I need to tell you that I had relations with my wife before we got married and I had never in my life done that before—not *ever*, even with Sandra What's-Her-Name! and it was *wonderful*, even though I stand the possibility of burning in Hell for it, and she ran away from me—Gail, not Sandra-- with the organist from our church and I sneaked out of a Diocesan meeting in Orlando to get a drink, which turned out to be a gay bar and somebody got *right in my face* and said, 'Are you tryin' to hit on *me*, you *Mother?*', even though I was not wearing my collar at the time or even thinking about hitting anyone, and I tried to explain that I was a Father, not a Mother, but somehow they knew I was not one of them and I am not sure I am one of *anyone* and I hate blue," I blurted out.

"Whoa! A little too much information there, Ollie!"

"But there is more! I was sitting on this barstool in this gay bar somewhere in Orlando all by myself, and I had sneaked away from my parishioners at the meeting because I thought the Bishop was looking at me funny— not ha ha funny, but—*disapproving* funny, you know?-- and I became aware that my barstool was wobbly. Did you get that, Oliver? It was *wobbly!*"

"I got it, man. That and not getting hit on as a straight Mother in a gay bar can really ruin your day."

"It *did!* I was getting so *mad* at that wobbly barstool that I yelled, 'Why cannot anything be right? *Black has to be black and white has to be white, not grey!* Why cannot even a barstool be even?' Huh—that is two 'evens' in the same sentence."

"Two evens—that's odd!" interrupted the woman with my other name, Georgina, who apparently had been continuing to listen in on this very private conversation, and she and Outrageous Oliver started to laugh before I could tell her how mightily offended I was at her for being such a Prying Polly.

"I am afraid that some people in the bar, both black and white, took offense at what they thought was a racist remark on my part, instead of just a quote from my high school teacher. At one point somehow I tried to fend off some female with my fists. At least I *think* it was a female. It was awfully dim in that bar, Oliver. I have to be honest here, Oliver. I grabbed at her hair and it came off!-- and I was face to face with the homeliest lady--! And then they helped me up off the floor."

"And what can I do about your confession, man?"

"Oh, Oliver, I need you to—I need you to forgive me. Will you forgive me, please? There is no one in this whole world who understands me the way you do. I have sinned, oh Oliver, I have sinned! And I wish they still said the word 'Propitiation' in the Comfortable Words, and you know that 'comfortable' comes from the Latin and means 'with strength', not comfy like a soft pillow, because I so would have liked to have been strong and said 'Propitiation" in front of a congregation and now somebody changed the Book of Common Prayer, so I cannot show people how to pronounce it correctly, you know?

"It is true that I have not loved God with my whole heart and I have not loved my neighbors as myself, because between you and me, Outrageous, I am kind of a snob—yes, I am! I *am* and I tend to think of myself as above other people and the people in my church seem to sense it and I do not know what to do about it, and I *so* want to know how to get along with them without losing myself, which as I said, is a bit of a snob who is afraid of hospital germs and elevators, oh Oliver. Oliver, I so very much need your forgiveness and your blessing. Will you please forgive me? Oliver to Oliver?"

The shameful part is that before I could receive Outrageous Oliver's blessing I dropped the phone and fell asleep.

George's Centre Cannot Hold. And yet . . . .

> "God, I can push the grass apart
> And lay my finger on thy Heart!"
> Edna St. Vincent Millay: Renascence

> (Miss Elliott's Favorite Lines,
> Added a Year later at Her Wedding
> and As a Favor to Her Father)

I have mislaid my journal. I have the key still around my neck, but the book itself has vanished.

Could Gail have taken it? No. I had it with me after she herself disappeared. I had it beside me on the front seat of the Chrysler just this morning, when I picked up Amber for school. And then I jotted down a few notes—

--or did I? I seem to be bungling times and places since losing Gail.

"Mother," I phone her, "has Amber come home from school?"

"Why, yes. Straight home on the school bus. She's such a good girl, George—you really need to pay more attention—"

"Mother. Listen carefully. This is important."

"Why—what is it, George? Have you heard from Gail?"

"No. That is not it. Look, can you see Amber's backpack?"

"Oh, I don't know—let me look around." I hear her drop the receiver onto the table and I put my hand to my wrist, the left one still holding the phone, and I try taking my pulse, even though that wrist is in the air, the phone to my ear, and I am not sure a pulse can be taken this way, but I am sure it is pounding away and that cannot be very healthy—

"George? Are you there?"

"Yes, Mother."

"It's here, under the table."

"All right. Good. Now Mother, where is Amber?"

"Oh—she's in her room. She's got music on. That means she's studying. George, how a person can study with all that noise is beyond—"

"Mother. Listen. I need you to go through the backpack and see if my journal is inside."

"Your--? Have you lost your journal? The one about St. Swithun's?"

"I'm sure it is not *lost.*"

"You—you think *Amber* took it? Why would she do a thing like that?"

"Mother, *please*! Will you just look?"

"Well—I just don't want her to catch me doing this. It's hard to build a child's trust, you know, George, especially when her own mother has abandoned her like this—"

"Nobody has abandoned anyone! I just need to—start eliminating places it might be."

"Oh." There is a pause as she puts the phone down. I am biting the skin inside my lips. "No. It's not here."

"Mother. Did you try all the pockets, all the--inside the lining? Feel around! There might be secret hiding places in those things."

"George. I *told* you. It's not here."

"All right. All right." Inspiration hits. "Did she wear a jacket today? A jacket with pockets?"

"I don't think so." Another pause. "But, George, *you're* the one who drove her! Can't *you* remember what she was wearing? I swear, she was out of here in such a flash in the morning, hardly ate breakfast—"

I slump against the door frame. I will have to search the house again, and then the car—see if it might have slipped down between the cushions—

"I remember, George! She didn't wear a jacket! I remember because I told her the Weather Channel had just said there was a cold front coming and she said she'd be home before it showed up—"

"All right. Thank you, Mother."

"You can't always trust that Weather Channel, though. Remember they told us about when the hurricane of— was it 2012 or 2013—was predicted down here in Florida and how thankful we were that we were in Connecticut, and then it never came? And I had Emilio put up the hurricane shutters last September when that hurricane with the funny name was supposed to come through and it turned the other way, and then he just had to take them down again, not that he minded, but I felt like I had to give him a big tip for doing that--. George? Are you still there?"

I am still here. I am reduced today to writing my thoughts in a yellow-lined notebook which I cannot lock, although why I care I do not know, since there is no one at home anymore except myself.

"George, come to dinner again tonight. Here it is Monday and you have the week ahead of you—a vestry meeting and another meeting with the organ committee--"

The organ committee! Without Old Lee here I could push through any ideas I want. The thought cheers me briefly. That committee has been stalled for months now.

"It's odd that Gail ran away at the same time that Leland took sick. And then *Emilio* didn't show up this morning to take the trash to the curb and I had to do it myself. It's all very odd, George. It reminds me of when your father didn't come home, time after time. But we are born to suffer and we are born to forgive, I was raised to believe—"

"Mother," I say absently, "you would have made a wonderful Buddhist."

A new terrible idea has pushed the missing journal from my thoughts—Leland! Why had not this occurred to me? I need to call Leland! I can tell him I am just checking to see if he is any better and to ask him what happened to him, that when he called in sick at the last minute we would have had to hold a Sunday service with no music, except that Amber stepped up.

Yes, that is what I shall do. I will be solicitous and make sure that he is at home. I hope he is very ill. I hope he is all alone.

But what if *Gail* were to answer the phone? If she is with him, she might. What would I say? Would I demand she return to me, remind her of her sacred marital vows and her child, if not to her husband, and her duties, which are certainly more important than any fleeting pleasure with that--that *organist*!

Of course in the end I dared not call. The best thing was to keep all of this—unfortunate-- *situation* under control and under wraps. The fewer people involved, the better.

*   *   *

It is Monday evening and I am once again trying to eat Mother's dinner. I have spent the day pushing paperwork around and gazing without energy at the various pipe organ brochures I have accumulated. Mother regards me every now and then and sighs. Amber ignores me completely.

"Emilio called. He said he had such good news for me."

"Who, Mother?"

"Emilio. That nice young man who works here at the apartments. Do you know, George, we can even give him a grocery list and he'll go to Publix for us, or the pharmacy? Now, that man is a treasure. He and Lee helped me choose the paint colors for these rooms, you know."

"He's cute," says Amber. I cannot put a face to this Emilio. "Do you have to give him money to do the shopping?" I ask listlessly.

"He gives back *all* the change. Really, George, if you're going to sit like a lump I'm going to be sorry I asked you here for dinner. At least you could admire the sunset. This many floors up it's really spectacular."

I glance up and out her picture window. The sun going down west of Banana Bay would be interesting at any other time, but my head is swimming with unfinished business. "Amber."

"Yes?" Oh, look at her. How can she not be prostrate with grief at her mother's disappearance? You would think that all was calm in her teenage life. "I am looking for my journal—"

"I already asked her, George. She hasn't seen it."

"That old book that you write in, George?" Oh, will she *never* call me "Father"? Well, of course she does at church, but then she giggles: "I don't need to call you 'Father', do I, George? Everybody else calls you that."

I should be more firm with her. I should have been more firm with Gail. Maybe she would still be here.

"Yes. That old book."

"Hm-m-m. Nope. Can't help you there." I also never noticed before that Amber seems to prefer straws when she drinks and now she is making a loud slurping noise with it.

"Amber—"

"What? Oh. Sorry, Grandma Doris." Amber lifts the straw from her glass and sucks air through it. And how come Mother can be "Grandma", but I cannot be "Father"?

"It was good to hear from your mother, wasn't it, Amber, and to know she's all right—"

"*You heard from Gail?*" I all but shout. Both females stare at me, Mother wide-eyed and Amber with a smile of being one-up on me.

"Well, yes—just about two hours ago, wasn't it, Amber?" Amber has gone back to playing with her straw. "Didn't I tell you so? Amber said that she said she was thinking of calling you next. So I thought she had."

"No! She—maybe I was in the yard. And she called?"

"Poor George. Lost his journal *and* his wife."

"Amber. That will be enough. You can see that your stepfather is upset."

Amber gives a huge sigh. "She's okay. I mean, she called to talk to Grandma, but when I picked up the phone, she apologized to me and said she had to get away for the week end, and that she'd be back tomorrow or the next day."

Gail coming back! "Well—where did she say she is?" I cannot believe that Gail would call my mother and not me! The woman must have lost her mind!

"She said she was with the girls. Orlando or Miami. Someplace like that."

"What—what *girls?*"

"I told you, she's done this before, George. It's not a big deal. And she always brings me something nice. Maybe she'd bring you something, too, if you weren't always fighting."

"We do not fight--!"

"I've heard you too, George. When I lived in the rectory. Even from the other end of the house. I never heard you raise your voice like that when you were a boy."

"Mother—. Mother, what is this that I am eating?"

"Chicken quesadillas. Good, aren't they?"

I am now aware of the strong onion aroma rising from my plate. My eyes are watering and I have a strange new sensation of having to—burp! I turn accusingly to the two women, to cover my embarrassment. "You have never cooked anything like this before!"

"I got the recipe from Emilio. Good, isn't it?"

"Emilio! Who is this Emilio? No, It is *not* goo—". I take a long swallow of water. My tongue burns and I am sure there is acid reflux going on south of my throat, too—

"I'd like some more, please, Grandma Doris." Oh, I've never seen Amber act so politely. Something's up. Maybe she *knows* where her mother is, with the girls. Girls, indeed!--

"George—I said it's not right to raise your voice the way you do, to your own wife, Dearie."

I push away from the table. "I have to go. I have a sermon to write. Get your things, Amber, and—"

"Uh--I'm not going home." Amber looks to my mother for support.

"She can stay here as long as she wants, George. I told her so. I have the space. We're like a couple of old roommates here, aren't we, Amber?"

"No. I want you at home, where you belong."

"I'm staying here, George."

"You belong at home in your own bed. This is an imposition on my mother."

"George, you cannot be alone in a house with an underage child. It just wouldn't look right, and you have appearances to maintain."

I look at Mother. "Are you suggesting--?"

"Not at all. But others might be alarmed. You need to pay attention to what others are thinking."

"George," Amber gives me a look that flits so suddenly across her face that for a startling moment she is Gail. "George--are you afraid to be *alone?*"

I am suddenly, wearily done. I am through. I am too tired, exhausted to argue, to lecture. I just want to get home and lie down. I need a drink. Ah. Yes. That's what

I've been missing. Alone, my feet up, with a drink and a TV show just for me. Something mindless.

"All right, you two. Have it your own way. As you wish." I make my way to the door. My mother switches on a light for me. How did it get dark so soon?

"George," two women say in unison, both pleading. "Don't drink."

"Well, that is just the worst thing I could do right now, is it not?" I say in my most lofty professional voice. "I am appalled that you would even think that way. Good night."

If this were not such a small town, if I were not a priest, I could stop at a local bar and order a libation or two. But I have been called to a more worthy position in life. People might know me, might comment. So I wait impatiently at traffic lights until I am safe at home to open the bottle of Scotch I have hidden in my bookcase, behind the "Lives of the Saints" and "No Man (or Woman) is an Island".

There is no message on the answerphone from Gail.

Well. If Gail and Old Lee are off somewhere together—and all the evidence points in this direction—I may as well be as soothed as possible with her rash decision. Shopping indeed!

The Scotch helps a little. I fall asleep in my leather chair with one reading lamp on. I dream of Gail and Leland entwined together, her beautiful legs, one just a mite shorter (although she denies this) than the other, clutching his hips and his back, her mouth seeking his male parts in a way I was reluctant to allow her to do with mine. Why? Was she asking too much? Should I have let her-- wantonness have its way with me?

"It's as though you're naked, but you're still wearing your collar, George," she breathes on me. And now oh, my God!-- *Leland* is touching me, rubbing my chest, my head, my feet. I must get away! He smiles knowingly at me—we share a precious woman, George. George. George.

I awake with a very dry mouth and an esophagus full of bile. My bladder aches as though it has been punched and I fall painfully onto my knees as I trip over a hassock in the dim light. It is as black as a heretic's soul out there in the world, where Gail is lost with her lover.

Oh! Will morning *never* come?

Whereupon George Regrets that He Wished for the Morning to Come

"Shame on us, Christian brothers, His name and sign who bear,

O shame, thrice shame upon us, to keep Him standing there!"

William Walsham How: Hymn 407, 1940 Episcopal Hymnal,

"O Jesus, Thou art standing Outside the fast-closed door"

I am having a difficult time opening my eyes, but I must stop that annoying tapping.

And then I realize someone is knocking on my front door. I am still in my clothing from yesterday and I have a powerful need to void. The phone is off the hook. I replace it, weak with fear that Gail might have tried to call me and found something wrong with the phone. I stumble to the door and open it—*Gail?* It must be Gail!

Mr. Campbell and two other members of the vestry—Miss Elliott and Mr. Foster-- look solemnly at me. It appears Miss Elliott is trying not to cry. My God—Gail! Gail is dead! That whoremaster Leland Frye has done away with her! I knew he was a criminal the first time we met!

"Uh-h--," is all I can say. Where is my tongue? It feels like sawdust in my mouth.

Mr. Campbell, always the gentleman, asks me, "Father George? Would you like to freshen up some? It seems we have caught you by surprise."

It looks as though this trio is not going to go away, so I retreat to my bathroom and make myself look as presentable as possible. It cannot be Gail, I decide, or there would be wailing. They all *like* Gail. Hah!--they will not, after they find out about her and Leland!

If it is *Leland* who is dead, then they need to be rejoicing. I *knew* he was no good from the minute I laid eyes on him!

I smell coffee when I enter the great room wearing a clean set of clothing and a fresh shave. Someone has poured me a glass of orange juice, which I sip carefully. Then Miss Elliott—"I brought you some homemade blueberry muffins, Father,"—takes the glass to the kitchen. Blue. To match the blue glow in the room.

"I just want coffee, thank you, Miss Elliott."

The group arranges itself around the dining table. I steel myself. "If this is about Gail--."

"No, not at all," Mr. Campbell says quietly.

"Then Mr. Leland Frye!"

"This is about *you*, Father," says Mr. Foster, his voice even more stern-sounding than usual.

"Yes?"

"Please sit back down, Father. Unless you'd rather be on the sofa."

"No. This will do." I do not deserve to be any more comfortable than this, until I get Gail safely home with me.

"Father George, we are aware that you have a drinking problem."

"Mr. Foster! Where did you hear a rumor like that?"

"On the radio Sunday night. On Outrageous Oliver's show. Miss Peabody heard it in rehab. The therapists were listening to it and laughing."

"She called me immediately," interjects Mr. Campbell. "She was so worked up, it still being the Lord's day and all. And then I called the others."

"But that's beside the point. You're an alcoholic, Father," says Mr. Foster. Miss Elliott sniffles in the background. "We had no idea, of course, when we hired you, and then when it became obvious from the get-go, we petitioned the Bishop."

"The Bishop--!"

"Well, that was no help. The Bishop told us that you apparently had something you were dealing with and that we would just have to work through it with you."

There is a sound at the front door—*Gail!*-- and before anyone can get up, Gladys Hitchcock and Mother enter. I gape. Mother's face is dark in a way I remember her being with my father, but never with me.

"George! How could you! I just found out about your radio escapade on Sunday night. George, whatever possessed you?"

"Mother, this is all so unfair--!" I begin. Mr. Foster, with his deeper voice, interrupts us.

"Mrs. Dudley, excuse me, but we have other matters going on here right now." He turns to me. "So we decided two things. We called your last parish and somebody there admitted they were glad to see you go because of your drinking—"

"This is preposterous!"

"George, let him finish. Please."

"Mother, I cannot believe you would be a party to this travesty!"

"—then we took a vote and decided we needed to send the Bishop a message about what was going on here, and we all decided to change our annual pledges to *one dollar*."

"When the Bishop saw that we couldn't afford you, George, and that we were even willing to go back to mission status, he changed his mind and told us all right, he'd replace you."

"Then he changed his mind again—he was *really* mad at us, Father George, for kinda goin' over his head!"

"Well, I should think so! Where is the respect he--?"

"And he arranged that St. Swithun's would go back to mission status immediately."

"So we have a supply priest set to come in on Sundays and all else is being referred to St. Barnabus' rector to handle."

"Now, Father George--we have a car ready to take you to the treatment center where the diocese sends church workers with problems."

I look at Mother. Her face is pale. "Oh, George. I'm sorry I didn't say something sooner."

"But do you all not understand what is going on with me, under the circumstances? *My wife has run off with Mr. Leland Frye!*"

The little group exchanges stunned looks. "Father George," says Mrs. Hitchcock firmly, "Leland is back."

"With Gail!"

"No. They never were together." Oh. I see it all now. This lynching party has made up a wild tale about the Bishop and my drinking and Leland and Gail, and has gotten my mother to go along with it, somehow. My mother has been brainwashed into blowing my little chat (which I do not even remember, so I really cannot argue with them about it) on the radio all out of proportion. Somehow this has to be Leland's doing!

"You are all crazy. I am not going anywhere!"

"Suit yourself, Father." Mr. Foster leans calmly over me, despite Mr. Campbell's efforts to hold him back. "But then you're not going to be our rector and we're not going to pay you a salary and you can't live here anymore. Be smart about this now."

I consider. Miss Elliott kindly brings me a fresh cup of coffee and two aspirins. How did she know I needed those?

"But how will Gail find me?"

"Gail knows where you are. She didn't want to be here this morning—"

"THEN WHERE THE HELL IS MY WIFE?" I shout. Miss Elliott jumps.

"George—she's moved in with Mrs. Hitchcock for a while." Mother has started to cry. "She's afraid to come back to you."

So while I was dining at Mother's last evening and being poisoned with onions, my wife was hiding in the same building, just one floor down, at Gladys Hitchcock's? I am, I fear, in some terrible science fiction movie. All those around me are messing with my brain, even Mother.

"It's true, Father," says Mrs. Hitchcock.

I turn on her: "This is all because Officer Robbins would not let me near your grandson until it was too late, is it not?" Oh, I understood now. This was bad—the legal system was in on it, too. No wonder the policeman had acted toward me the way he had—

Mrs. Hitchcock gasps.

"You stepped on him, George!" Mr. Foster growls. "You were so drunk that you *stepped* on him!" Now Mrs. Hitchcock and Mother are both crying and Miss Elliott has turned away from us.

"Well," I say, trying desperately to make sense of all these lies, "I see I have no choice except to go along with you all." ("You all". Oh no. Are they turning me into a Southerner? Were those really aspirins Miss Elliott handed me, or something more mind-bending?)

The group lets out a collective breath. "He's going to be fine, Mrs. Dudley," says Mr. Campbell. "How about you pack his things? You know what he'll need."

There has to be an explanation for all of this, I think wildly. I feel like a tiger in a cage. What would get them

all so riled up? And then I have it: they have read my--
"*Which one of you stole my journal?*" I shout now. I feel for my key. Ah! It is still around my neck. But they could have removed it while I was sleeping! "You shall not get away with it, you know. And you know who you are!"

"Nobody knows a thing about that, Father."

"It just seems preposterous to lose Gail and Mr. Frye *and* my journal all in the same day—"

"Not to mention losing your church," says Mr. Foster grimly. He never liked me, I think. I can see that now. I should have let him sing more solos. What other enemies have been in my midst?

Mr. Campbell opens the front door. There is, to my utter alarm, a car with an unknown driver waiting outside. *They really mean to do this!* I think fearfully, and I only stop shaking a little when Miss Elliott takes my arm. I am in the back seat of the car with a suitcase and my briefcase with the G.O.D. initials on it before I know what is happening. Mother has kissed me and hugged me. The rest have stood there silently, guarding the rectory against my re-entry.

Miss Elliott drops a little package into my lap. "The rest of the muffins," she whispers. "To remind you of us and your home here."

I am whisked away before I can quite figure out what has happened. I stare through the windows to catch a glimpse of Gail, but they are holding her someplace away from me.

Well. Since they are all telling me lies I have nothing to do except go along with their charade until I can get my wife back.

The last person I gaze with astonishment upon at St. Swithun's is Mr. Leland Frye, who is standing on the church steps with a young black-haired man. The both look cheerful for some unknown reason. To show that I am above all this and do not suspect anything about the organist's surely-nefarious doings, I wave jauntily at him the way the Queen would.

**Whereupon George learns that
The Reason Dudley Do-Right's
Rear End didn't Hurt was because
He was just a Cartoon Character**

"Go get water, water is good to drink;
Water will drown better than wine will drown
Certain sorrows that refuse to go down. . .
Stick your hand in the stream;
Water will run and kiss it like a dog."
Merrill Moore: Hymn For Water
(Moore was a psychiatrist, an authority on alcoholism,
and wrote more than 30,000 sonnets.)

"You have a visitor, Father George," says the very young reception person.

My first visitor!

"Dr. Alberta says it's ok."

It has to be Mother. Or Gail. But it is neither one. In the entrance hall stands a cowboy. He is about sixty or so, his face and hands weather beaten and tanned by the sun. He is lean and tall and wears a clean checked shirt, belt with a large brass buckle, and well-worn jeans and boots. He holds a cowboy hat in his grip. He looks across at me.

"Did you want me?" I ask, puzzled. There is another George here, I think—"

"Father George Dudley. You're the one I want." His voice is soft.

"But I'm afraid I don't—"

"They told me if I saw you I should listen close to make sure you're usin' contractions."

"Oh. That. Yes, they're turning me into a real sinner here."

"Got somethin' outside for you."

Gail? The receptionist nods her permission and we step outside onto the wide covered porch of the building which has been constructed like an old Cracker home. The pleasant March air drifts across my face.

I stop. Two huge horses are tethered to a post.

"Dr. Alberta says you allus wanted to be some guy called Dudley Do-Right. Don't know about him, but she said the guy rode a horse and you never had."

I stare up. The smaller horse's head looms over me. "Name's Betty. She's a good ole kind of horse. Good for a first ride."

He looks down at my sneakers. "Well, guess they'll do." I am wearing my first pair of jeans ever, sent in a kind of C.A.R.E. package by Mother, and a tee shirt given to me by my group with an inscription on the front: I NEVER MAKE MISTEAKS. I was told it is appropriate for me. In my darker moments it drives me wild.

"You got a hat? No? Yeah, I guess just sunglasses'll do."

The cowboy helps me up and shows me how to hold the reins—"Don't choke up on 'em, now. Don't keep yankin' at her. Let 'em go kinda slack. Nice and easy. She needs to get the feel of your partic'lar weight under her. "

Betty is as wide as a barrel. I sit straddled across an old leather saddle as my—those things I put my feet in—are adjusted. One ride is sure to make me bowlegged! I worry momentarily about my vulnerable male parts.

The cowboy mounts his horse in an easy movement, one he has apparently been doing all his life. Good thing I have come to expect about anything in my weeks here. Anything, that is, except Mother and Gail.

I see with a jolt that I have thought of Mother first. Amber has written me every week, but the notes are cursory: "I have a new boyfriend, I hate my gym teacher, Grandma Doris says I'm on my cell phone all the time and my music is too loud, but what else is there to do?" No details about Gail, which I find frustrating, except for one piece of information: Leland and his boyfriend Emilio hopped across state lines to get married legally.

All right, I told my group when I found that out, so I was guilty of a small bit of irrational thinking, but so would they, under the same circumstances! This was when they all threw Nerf balls at me, as a reminder to quit assuming.

Betty bumps along. "You're doin' fine," the cowboy tells me. "Betty's taken to you like you been ridin' her for years." I beam with pride. He sits straight in his saddle, he and his horse seeming to have one mind between them. *I'm Dudley Do-Right!* I think.

"Excuse me, but are you part of the group experience?" I ask. He guffaws. I swear that is the correct word to use for his laugh.

"No, son, I'm here 'cause of St. Swithun's."

"Oh."

"Now, don't sound so dejected. I have a story to tell you, but go easy on this part of the trail. Don't want to stir up any rattlers."

"S-snakes?"

"They tend to make a horse bolt. Just foller me, now."

I am more than glad to. We are back in the part of Florida that tourists never see, the old Florida of the Crackers and the cowboys. The land stretches to the horizon, with hammocks-- large patches of raised pieces of land and trees, mostly slash pines and Sabal palms-- dotting the area. The air is fresh with none of last summer's burnt heavy feel. Betty is sure-footed and steady underneath my buttocks. My guide does not make any idle conversation. I am relieved to be outside and away from the constant caring psychological pounding that I have been receiving. Two buzzards circle overhead in lazy patterns and I almost fall off Betty, tipping back to watch them. There's no sound of cars, and even a plane going somewhere is so high up that it can't be heard. I sigh, relaxing.

"Are you," I venture to ask, "a Cracker?" I have learned that this is not an insulting term: the Crackers were early settlers who had big bullwhips and when they whipped them through the air, the sound was that of a "crack".

"Yep. Florida native." He passes me, oddly enough, a Publix plastic bottle of water. I would have expected a hide-covered flask. "Make sure you don't leave that behind, now."

"Thanks," I say gratefully. I realize now how thirsty I am. The sun warms my back under my sports shirt.

Most of the group I have met and lived with have gone back to their homes. There's been a new batch of clergy, men and women from all over the United States, show up, in various forms of denial. *Lord, was I ever like that?* has been my first thought, and then my second one of both warmth and pity. *We're all survivors here.*

"Mind tellin' me who you are? You seem t' know who I am." His dialect is rubbing off on me.

"Well, George, your organist told me I need to level with you."

"*Leland?*"

"Miss Peabody. Here it is: I'm Miss Harriett Peabody's natural son. That's the long and short of it and there's no other way to put it."

"Wait! You're—what?"

"Funny that nobody ever put two and two together. Edith Hatcher sendin' Miss Peabody all those letters braggin' so much about her famous St. Swithun's, you know. And the will written in the Bible."

"Sure. That's how all the flap about the church color came from."

"But the truth is there never *was* an Edith Hatcher."

I almost fall off Betty at this news. "But the letters--!"

"Miss Peabody made 'em all up. Anybody actually *see* those letters? Thought not."

"But—why?"

"Far's I can tell, she went kinda stir crazy for a while, bein' pregnant and all. Her folks whisked her out of town 'til I was born and giv' up for adoption to some really nice folks. She had nothin' else to do while waitin', so she read nothin' but romance magazines and then she made up a bunch a' letters."

"Wow," I said softly.

"Yep. She told me she felt like such a nobody and all her growin' up years she'd wanted to be somebody. The boy who was my natural father, he was an exchange student from England; never knew what he'd done and she never told him, and that kinda ate away at her. And a'course, as I got older and had me a wife and family, the desire grew in me to know my real parents, not just the good ones who had raised me. They told me about my natural Ma and that she was still at St. Swithun's, so my daughter and I visited there a few times, way before you ever showed up. That's when I found Miss Peabody and I told her who I was. A'course, she first denied it. I was in the hospital visitin' her when you showed up there one day—remember?"

I think back. The man with the cowboy hat in his lap—this same man!

"She was so fulla pain pills that she spilled the whole story."

"But—but the letters! And the *blue*!"

"Like I said, nobody ever saw those letters 'cept the coupla ones Miss Peabody showed 'em. That's 'cause there weren't any from any real Edith Hatcher. Miss Peabody wrote the will herself, in the back of an old Bible she found in the thrift shop. Put Edith Hatcher's name on the front. Who'd think to check? Who'd doubt Miss *Peabody*, after all those years at church and all the letters she'd read to everybody about life at St. Swithun's?"

"*Is* there a real St. Swithun's?"

"Sure is. You can find it today on the computer at Wick-ee-peedia, she told me. I did. She got her facts right. A'course, *she* used books instead, while she was waitin' for me to be born. She did some research into obscure places and schools and hit on this one."

"But still—blue! Why do *that*?"

"Not so hard to understand. Here you have an old lady, been playin' faithfully all those years, writin' fake letters jest to please herself and have the last laugh, and year after year just scrapin' by, with the vestry vetoin' any liveable pay raise for her all that time. They figured since she wasn't complainin' too loud, that she was doin' the job out of the kindness of her heart. Well, she finally got so fed up pleadin' with 'em and gettin' nowhere that she hit upon the church paintin' story."

"Wow. Incredible. But how about the grandfather who donated the land for the church?"

"Oh, a man *did* that. But he wa'n't a grandfather. His name was Winchester. Old bachelor. No living relatives. Nobody to confirm or deny my Ma's stories."

"Incredible," I repeated.

"What's incredible's the *next* part—the church loved the name St. Swithun's and they loved the idea of an annual festival so much that every year Miss Peabody has to suffer with her lie by watchin' everybody be so happy about bein' blue."

I don't know what to say. All those years of anger building up in that poor woman . . . .

"It was *you* changed her, Father George. You and your confession on the rad-dio."

"Me? How?"

"She told me, 'If my own priest can repent and need confession, then so can I.' "

"I—I don't even remember—"

"Son, it doesn't matter. Your little church has more new people in it now, people who heard that rad-dio show and felt such sympathy for you. You got *real* that night, Father."

"Did they send you to tell me that?"

"I live here. You're on my property, son. This dryin' out place is part of my acreage, here in Kissimmee."

I could now see familiar buildings ahead of us far off in the distance. We must have ridden for miles in a huge circle, I thought.

"There's more you might want to know—I went to the courthouse and demanded my rights as Harriett Peabody's natural-born son. She loved me doin' that. While you was busy spillin' your beans that Sunday night, I was gettin' a calf birthed. Heard you on the rad-dio in the barn. Nearly dropped the calf."

"Oh, Lord. You too?"

'Your own Ma didn't hear it first-hand. Be grateful. Anyway, while you was in here puttin' yourself back together, I was gettin' the church painted white. Took five coats. And that's *after* they sand-blasted it. Oh, yeah, they hadda go buy a new organ, too. The old one just burned itself out one day. Wasn't Miss Amber's fault a'tall. Wonder she didn't get hurt. They gotcha a nice Allen organ with that stop you wanted."

An Allen—well, if it had to be electronic—wait! Did he mean Leland had given in on the Gambe stop? All at once it didn't matter. "Stop! One thing at a time! Why cover up the blue?"

" 'cause sometimes I take things personally and sometimes I don't. I hope you're learnin' the difference in this place. I took that blue color personally. That blue color, it just wa'n't right for the House of the Lord."

"It was like she was screaming to the world, 'I had a baby boy!' " I mused.

"Huh," said the cowboy. "That's what a coupla months of pop psychology in this place'll do to you. Nossir, she hated all what had happened to her so bad it's a wonder she didn't have the flag a' England painted there on the church."

He let his horse stop for some grass and I let Betty do the same thing. Actually, Betty did the stopping herself.

Boy, am I kidding myself, I thought—I think I'm ordering my horse to do something and she's already made up her mind what she wants to do. And then I take credit for it. Is that what I have been doing all my life—pretending to lead? Just *pretending*, going through the motions?

"Nossir." The cowboy was still musing. "Miss Peabody felt so bad after your confessin' that she told me to go ahead and get that church painted over."

"She had us believing that Edith Hatcher was like a— little Hitler," I mused, remembering uncomfortably what Gail had called me once.

"People needin' power and control don't do much damage to others—unless they got lots of money. Miss Peabody didn't have much, and yet she was willin' to use it all up just to get back at the vestry. She prob'ly only had enough to paint it blue one more time, and then they would have found out."

"So all the bragging about Edith Hatcher's school—," I said.

"—was by a person who never saw it herself. My natural Ma was so ashamed of that, didn't never want anybody to find out. Until you came along. Watch it."

Betty shies away from a snake. "Black racer. Harmless. Don't know how Betty tells the difference, but she does. Maybe the harmless ones smell different from the poisonous ones."

"If only people were like that," I say.

"You gotta ease up on the reins with people, son. They don't take much for bein' controlled. Ever had a dog or a cat for a pet?"

"Mother said they were too much trouble."

"That's a pity. Person learns a lot about himself, takin' care of an animal. Well now, I have both. Now you take my good old faithful dog Muttley out to my truck and the dog gets all excited: 'Oh boy, we're goin' for a ride!' Take my *cat* out to the truck and she starts howlin', 'Oh no! I'm gonna *die*!' Same with people. Use a heavy hand and some people might go along, but most'll be like my old black cat Desmond."

"But, well, okay—I hate to admit it, but every evening when we have dinner I'm automatically looking around for people who might need help; like if they should drop a utensil or a napkin, then I could get it for them. But then I miss the conversations."

"Well, Father George, Dr. Alberta told me that ole Dudley Do-Right of yours went lookin' for people to help, even when they didn't need it."

"Well, sure—they just didn't know they *needed* help."

"It's kinda easy helpin' others instead of seein' if you can use the help yourself."

"The way Miss Peabody—your Ma-- did," I mused.

"Like *you* did. *You* got a fine bunch of people waitin' for you to come back to them, so's they can help *you*. You done some miracles there, son."

Without warning, Matt's sunny freckled face as he tinkered with Mother's car appears before my eyes along with the cowboy's kindly one. I start heaving huge sobs. I want to stop, but can't. Betty halts and I lean down and put my arms around her neck and mane, as far as I can reach, and I cry the way my group has been urging me to do and I have been resistant to. The cowboy moves off a bit so that I can be alone. There is no sound except for my sobbing. I recall the day of Matt's funeral when Amber climbed into my arms. I cry for my father and his own dreams for me, my making snobbish fun of him; for Mother and her willingness always to be there for me, and Gail, whom I used for my own pleasure without ever finding out what *her* dreams were; poor Miss Peabody, carrying her burdens alone; the congregation that I let down; and for myself and the skinny insecure little kid that I was.

Finally I am spent and am heaving great sighs. I can hardly open my eyes. The cowboy returns, looks me over briefly, clucks to Betty, and we head on.

Back at the front porch of the group meeting house the cowboy helps me slide down from my horse. I am having a hard time standing up, let alone walking. "Fine ride," I manage to say, sticking my hand out to shake his. I am exhausted and thirsty and need to lie down. I can't remember ever having been this tired in my life. I also need to find Dr. Alberta and talk with her some more about what just happened to me. "Thank you, sir."

The cowboy nods briefly. Then a tough leathery hand grasps mine in a familiar grip, *the kind Jesus must have had*, I think suddenly with awe as a sort of electric shock goes through me. No soft palms for Him! He knew what hard work was like—I sit down hard on the porch step.

"You ok, son?" the cowboy asks.

"I was just—oh my!--just reminded of my father and how he used to hold my hand," I reply. A familiar gasoline and oil smell is suddenly in my nostrils, although there is not a car to be seen.

"Uh-- I don't even know your name and I need—if I may ask, what brought you here today?"

"Why, son—they thought maybe you'd like to come home."

Home! Where is home for me now? I rise rather painfully. "Oh, thank you, sir, but I've just discovered-- I have a little more work to do here before I can go leave."

"I'll come again, then." Now he smiles and that smile reminds me of someone, but I cannot remember who. He mounts his horse and then waves to me. "My daughter says to tell you hello."

Gail's father! I have been out riding with Gail's father, I want to believe. But the smiles don't match. It's someone else . . . and I suddenly smell blueberry muffins.

Homecoming

"come on! there's a whole universe next door. let's go."

e.e.cummings

(George may have also misquoted

Edward Estlin Cummings)

This is the day I have been both anticipating and dreading. Dr. Alberta will not let me stay any longer. "You can get addicted to this place as well as anything else, George. Remember that you have an addictive bunch of wires in your brain from before you were born and go easy on yourself."

The cowboy did not show up. Rather, the same man who had driven me here is driving me home, and look at where I have been living! Just a short way from Disneyworld! Just far enough away not to see the lights or hear the nightly fireworks. Two different worlds.

My driver speaks for the first time. "Need to stop for anything? We have over an hour's drive ahead of us."

I have a huge overwhelming need to rush home, grab up Gail in my arms and promise her the world. I need to tell her how much I've changed, how willing I am to help her discover herself, to stop being a weight around her, to get back to having some really good love-making--!

If I can find my wife after all this time without a word from her.

"Uh, thanks. I would like a cup of coffee. Real coffee." He obligingly moves through the first drive-through Starbucks that we see and I order a scone as well. I'd like to talk some more, just to take some of my tension away, but he turns up the radio and we listen to country music for the rest of the drive to Banana Bay.

I'm just beginning to understand why a man would cry over the loss of his pickup and his dog when the car brakes to a stop in Holopaw, halfway to Banana Bay, in front of a rundown tavern with the unoriginal name of "Dewdrop Inn".

"What--?"

"You are expected. I'll wait. Go inside."

This is someone's idea of a joke, or a test. I am some months sober and the first thing I do with my freedom is get ushered to a bar. But my driver seems determined, so I get out of the car and go inside.

The first thing that hits me is the smoke, so much that the room has a bluish cast to it. It is like a little glimpse of hell after my stay at the monkish drying-out ranch in the wilderness.

The second is the music, if that is what it can be called. To my church chorale-trained ears it's perfectly dreadful. Three huge men, one with a guitar, one with a bass viol and one at the drums are arguing fiercely—apparently the one will win who has the loudest voice. Or the biggest beer belly, since they seem ready to push at each other like Sumo wrestlers.

And then, emerging from the men and the smoke, is—*Gail*.

At least I *think* it's Gail, it's so dark in here. This woman is wearing a long blonde wig, the shortest black leather skirt without displaying her crotch that I've ever seen, and of all things—white go-go boots left over from the past four decades.

"Hello, George," this woman says to me.

It is my wife.

"C'mon, sit down over here," she says, propelling me with her hand. "Gotta take time out, fellas!" she shouts to the erstwhile musicians. I find I am speechless.

"Cute, huh?" she says, sitting me at a table and twirling around in front of me. "The guys thought it up. Kinda like Fay Wray, you know, remember?"

"What--?"

"Hey. *You* look different. That place you were at did you a world of good." Before I can think of what to say, she says, "George. I'm sorry for running out on you like that."

"Amber said you went with the girls to Orlando or Miami—"

"Oh!" she laughs. I told her I went with the *Gorillas*, George. My band! Remember Gail and the Gorillas? Well, you were getting drunk so much and your mother was being so good with Amber and things at least with her were calm, that I thought I'd look up my old group again. And *George*--!" I try to stare at her, blinking my eyes from all the smoke—"they had just fired their old singer for drugs or something, and I sang with them that night and I was *great*, George! Oh-h-h!"

 The memory lights up her face. "Plus that other girl they had, she never liked being called 'Gail'. How about that, George? They even left my name in—'Gail and the Gorillas'. That's a sign, right?"

She starts to light up a cigarette and then stops. "Uh uh. Bad for my voice." I don't comment on all the secondhand smoke she is ingesting into her lungs (and mine) as we sit here.

 "I'm sorry, George. I just wasn't that happy being married. Nothing personal—but I just had to get out and find my dream."

"This—this is your *dream?*"

"Well, not all of it—I mean, the wig gets heavy after I've been wearing it all night and I miss Amber every now and then—but I'm on the *road*, George! I'm on the road, just like Lady Gaga!" Her face shines with happiness.

"But—but we're married!"

"Oh, yeah, about that. Well, your Mr. Foster found me a lawyer and he drew up some papers and all you have to do is sign them when you get back. Nothing ventured, nothing lost, right, George?"

" 'Nothing ventured, nothing gained' ." She stares at me and then laughs. "Oh! You always were a great one for correcting my English!"

"But we're *married*."

"Yeah, well, George—why don't we just look on it as kind of a *trial* marriage, not a real one."

"We were married in a *church*."

"It was just a piece of paper, George."

"But I don't see how—"

"*You were lousy at sex*, George! What can I tell you?"

And just like that something snaps inside me and I feel released. I stand up. "Well, thank you, Gail. It's been a real—experience."

"Wait, don't go! You haven't heard me sing yet. We're about to rehearse."

"A driver is waiting for me."

"Oh. Well, then--." She has turned back to her Gorillas and I wonder what ever prompted me to marry her in the first place. Then I see she is limping a little—possibly one of those Gorillas stepped on her foot—and to my amazement I feel no need, *none at all*, to be Dudley do-Right.

I head for the door. Her hand is all at once on my shoulder. "George," she says. "I prayed for you every night. Because if not for you I wouldn't be here now."

"Powerful prayers, those," I say and find that I can smile. "Good-by, Gail."

She leans over and kisses me. " 'bye, George."

And just like that I am outside gulping in the blessed Florida fresh air, perfumed with orange blossoms, and feeling a searing regret; but no need for a drink. And look at how close I was to one! All of ten feet to the bar rail! Dr. Alberta would be so proud of me.

*   *   *

The next stop is at Mother's. The driver lets me off at her apartment building. Everything looks so bright and shiny and clean—the grass clipped, the plants thriving. Green, green Florida—how happy I am to be living here! If I were up north I'd be waiting to see if another freeze was going to hit before spring really appeared.

Down here Banana Bay is riotous with color, obscene with aromas, the trees alive with mockingbirds. I whistle to one and it answers in kind.

"Better wait, in case she's not home," I tell my driver and he nods.

I enter the elevator and take a deep breath. You're ok, you're ok, I tell myself. And I am.

Someone must have informed Mother that I was coming; she opens the front door before I can knock. She is wearing a new pants outfit and has had her hair done, I can see. She hugs me tightly. "You look so good, George!"

"You too! New glasses?" I hang onto her. "I'm so happy to see you, Mother."

"I love you, too, George. Oh my, you haven't seen my place since I had it repainted. Oh, so much has happened! And I thought that maybe if I had my apartment painted I might grow to like it more, but I've gotten to thinking lately that I just don't like *heights*."

"I saw Gail."

"Oh. Yes. I'm sorry. They said you would."

"It's all right, Mother. It's all right. Now—where's Amber?"

"Why, she doesn't live here anymore."

She couldn't possibly be on the road with Gail and the Gorillas! Living that kind of life--!

"She's in Arkansas with Gail's sister. That's where she always goes when Gail runs away. You know Gail has this bad habit of running away."

"Not until recently. Ah. Poor Amber."

"She left you her address, in case you want to write to her."

"Of course I'll write to her."

My mother goes to the kitchen counter and picks up a piece of paper.

"Hm-m. She wrote down 'Father George'. That's a good sign."

"I'm just about ready, George. Just let me get my wrap."

"Why did you have your place re-painted?" I call to her.

"Ed thought it looked garish and tacky, and you know, George, it *was*."

"Who's Ed?"

"Oh. Just a man I know. He was the one who found a job for Joyce, our building's new landscape architect, after Emilio--."

"Landscape architect? You mean Joyce is the one who mows the lawn in front of your building. What happened to Emilio?"

"Oh—he's gone. Come on, George. Want to freshen up in the bathroom? I don't want to be late. Oh my, you look good. So rested and—I don't know—different, somehow."

"I'm sober," I say as I head down the hall.

Outside, the car is gone. In its place stands a big beat-up looking truck. "Where are we headed?" I ask.

"Not us, George. Just you. I'm riding with Gladys." Oddly, Mother has acquired an orchid corsage while I was in the bathroom. She waves me off and I climb into the truck. I tell the driver, "This is the first time in my entire life that I have ridden in a truck."

"Well, son, I hope it's not your last," says my driver, the cowboy. I am ceasing to be surprised at this day's unfolding.

"Mother told me trucks were dangerous."

"So is everything in life, but you can't just wrap yourself in a cocoon and wait it out."

"Have you ever—been in an accident?"

"Yep. Some of 'em not my fault." I let go further inquiry. I am up pretty high here, bouncing along as I did on Betty. The truck smells faintly of manure and fresh grass. I am busy looking at the streets of Banana

Bay, so clean and tropical, when I notice that we are on Winchester Street.

I am taken aback as we pull up to the church—it's now *white* and seems to settle down into the ground, where before it looked as though it was going to take off like a pointed blue balloon.

"Oh," I breathe. "It's lovely."

The rectory has been painted also, and it's a pale sandy color. I'm sorry I'll never get to live there again. Maybe they'll sell me the leather chair. Well, my actions have caused the Bishop to have made that decision for me.

"Suit you, Father George?"

"The church and the rectory are beautiful," I tell him. "How did you possibly manage this?"

"You want to see the organ first? Make sure it's got that gamb-y thing you wanted?"

"No, I can wait." (Yes, I realize, I can. Also, I am not prepared to meet Leland Frye.) "But the paint color—how did you get past the will and the court?"

"Well, you remember how the Bishop took us back to mission status after we called him about you?"

"Yes."

"Well, see, the imaginary Edith Hatcher's will called for having a blue church. But we weren't a *church* anymore, y'see. The Bishop had called us a mission and we weren't about to argue with him."

"Oh! Now wait a minute-- that's—that's a far stretch of semantics."

"Mebbe. But nothin' was ever said about a blue *mission*."

I shake my head and laugh. "But—but one lie doesn't justify another one--!"

"Father George, quit blusterin'—you gotta sometimes just lie back and enjoy God's benefits."

We are, I see, heading over the causeway with its high rise bridge. A mile in front of us the Atlantic Ocean shimmers in the sunlight. "Where are we heading?"

"To brunch, George." And to my amazement we drive up to the Banana Bay Yacht Club and Golf Course. A huge hand-lettered banner hangs over the front door: WELCOME HOME FATHER GEORGE. I am stunned.

"What in the world--?"

"Here you are. Last stop."

"Oh, but-- I'm not sure I'm ready to see anybody from St. Swithun's yet--."

But the cowboy has opened my truck door and is persistently pulling at me. Then the entrance door to the Yacht Club opens and people, some my parishioners, many not known to me, stream out, yelling, "He's here! HE'S HERE!" and they are clapping me on the back and hugging me and kissing my cheek and even ruffling my hair, and at the end of the line I spot Mother, her orchid flopping around on her shoulder.

She stands next to Miss Elliott, who is laughing, applauding and crying at the same time. The cowboy walks over and kisses the younger woman on the cheek. *Ah*, finally I notice. Their smiles are the same. Miss Elliott and the cowboy are father and daughter.

*   *   *

"Your last name must be Elliott," I say to him, shouting over the crush of people. Miss Peabody sits playing away quite loudly at the grand piano in the main room and we all have to talk over her crashing chords. There must be, according to the number of prepared tables, at least a hundred people here. Why, I think, that's more of St. Swithun's than I have ever seen!

"First name's Tom," he says, shaking my hand in that grip I remember. "You have my daughter to thank for these arrangements. We were just gonna have a reception in the parish hall, but she said you'd never had a chance to have brunch here, because you were always givin' your sermon at that time of day."

"How did she know that? And how did she manage to secure this—?"

"Not a problem, son. I'm one of the foundin' fathers of this here club." We are now sitting at a long table,

Mother on one side of me and Miss Elliott on the other. Her father sits next to her, and the vestry members have taken the other seats. Mother has removed her corsage. "It's lovely and thank you," she has said to a man nearby, "but it itches."

"Where are all the children?" I ask Miss Elliott.

"They're having lunch in a separate room here. We've got a movie and games for them and a magician. Their parents are delighted."

"I can't believe—what must all this be costing the church--?"

"After the speeches and the welcome homes, we're all going back to the church. You drove past it, didn't you? Good. Isn't it gorgeous, all white?" announces Mrs. Hitchcock. She invites a round of applause for Tom Elliott. "We're all set up for your first Eucharist service back, Father."

"Oh. I'm—I'm not sure—I don't even have the proper suit on."

"We never know what you're wearing under your vestments, anyway, Father." And here Mrs. Hitchcock puts her hand over her mouth at the thought.

Mr. Campbell chimes in, "We do have one favor to ask, though. And Mr. Tom here has given it his approval, so we just need yours."

"And that is--?"

"We want to keep on celebrating St. Swithun's Day. Even though the church isn't blue anymore. Shi—sorry, Father—shoot, that's what we're known for in Banana Bay—all our blue food!"

I look at Tom Elliott, who is preoccupied in listening to his daughter.

There is a little scuffle at the microphone and Miss Peabody, wearing an eye-numbing purple floral printed kind of muu-muu emerges victorious. "I have something to say and then I'm going to pass the microphone around so you can join in," she announces, her voice echoing throughout the pecky cypress-lined room. I glance outside through the floor-to-ceiling windows at the moored yachts bobbing in the Indian River. I sigh, so happy to be here and so painfully aware that this surreal Florida job must end.

"I was a very angry person for years. I don't know if you knew that," she scowls at the assemblage. "That is, until the night I was at rehab after I fell on that damned Cat-Mandoo, God rest his or her sorry soul."

Mr. Foster tries to take the mic away and she resists successfully with a jab of her good elbow. "I was at rehab when I heard Outrageous Ollie's show and our own Father George phoned in. I never realized a *priest* could use confession until I listened to him—it was mightier than any sermon he'd ever preached!"

"Amen!" shouts someone in the crowd.

"Well, I felt like getting down on my knees then and there, but I couldn't—I was in rehab!" she shouts, despite the mic. "And I figured if *he* could confess, then so could I. So I started truth-telling you all that there never was an Edith Hatcher or any letters. And I don't know why I started that lie, but I was just fifteen years old at the time and I needed to lash out at the world and I sure couldn't brag about myself, not after what I had let happen to me, so I figured I'd let Edith brag *for* me."

The response is so low-key that I understand—they have all been informed about this already. No surprises here, except to me. Even Mother wears an accepting expression.

"It was Father George over there who did it, who got me to finally tell the truth. And I want to tell you that the person responsible for getting the church repainted is my own son Tom Elliott!"

Tom waves at her from his seat beside Miss Elliott.

"I was brought up in a time of shame and denial, as though this could never happen. But if we don't admit the truth, then what chance do our children and grandchildren have?"

There is not only a round of applause, but people standing and cheering for her. She hands the mic to a young man before Mr. Foster can take it away from her. It is now being passed around the room, to people I have never seen before.

"I was in a heap of bar fights until I heard Father George's confession about he did the same thing, and it turned me around, and I decided I'd better come to St. Swithun's to see what this priest is all about." He hands the mic to another young man.

Good Lord! I had talked about a *bar fight* on the radio?

"Hi, folks. What a relief to be able to say I am gay and I'm so glad I have a church to go to where I can be myself." A couple of people at this young man's table clap him on the back. "When Father George accepted Lee Frye, I knew I was going to be safe."

But I didn't know about Lee! They're giving me credit where none is due!

"I've started a support group at church for unwed mothers," says an older woman. "I was one myself and I suffered in silence over this—thank you, Father George and Miss Peabody." More applause. I am stunned.

An old man stands up. "I was in the Freedom March, way back. Got thrown in jail for standing up for the truth, just like Father George did."

"That was St. Paul, not me!" I want to tell him, but the crowd is too noisy. The mic continues to be passed from table to table. So many people I have never seen before!

"My wife and I and our two teenagers have all joined the choir. We graduated years ago as music majors at

Florida State, but our kids want to Go Gators—can you believe that!"

A round of laughter. Real music people in the choir? I must be dreaming. The next rector will have a wonderful congregation to lead.

I feel a wave of resentment rise within me at the idea. Then I hear Dr. Alberta's voice: "Feel it, George, *feel* it. You don't have to act on it and drink, but you have to *feel*."

Mr. Campbell is now speaking: "About St. Swithun's Day Festival—do we continue it or not now, knowing there never was a real Edith Hatcher?"

There is a sudden uproar. Mother pushes at me with her elbow. "Do something, George," she hisses.

"I can't. These aren't—this isn't my church anymore. They're not going to listen to me."

Tom Elliott quiets the diners. "We need to hear from Father George. He's in charge, after all." To my surprise, the others nod and even the scowling Miss Peabody looks accepting. I stand up. Miss Elliott grips my hand for a moment.

"My friends, you all have an advantage over me. You have all experienced St. Swithun's Day and I have not. Miss Peabody, I grieve for the hurt you've carried alone all these years. You were not treated fairly. And perhaps every year there has been a new wound in your side with the festivities, every one so happy while you were the only one who knew the real person who had started all this." She nods.

"While I was drying out and being healed of my addiction to alcohol,"—there is a murmur among the parishioners— "Yes, I am an alcoholic. You all knew it before I did. I am recovering, not yet recovered. Our group said a prayer daily and I've been thinking about the imaginary Edith Hatcher. I daresay we all have an imaginary person inside us, telling us we're not good enough or beautiful enough or young enough or worthy enough. But we cannot let this tiny nagging voice rule our lives."

I pause to wait for the murmuring crowd to quiet. "Please bow your heads and let us pray." And I repeat the prayer I had said so many times with my therapy group:

"O blessed Lord, you ministered to all who came to you; look with compassion upon all who through addiction have lost their health and freedom. Restore to them the assurance of your unfailing mercy; remove from them the fears that beset them; strengthen them in the work of their recovery; and to those who care for them, give patient understanding and persevering love. Amen."

There is a resounding chorus of "Amen!"s.

Mr. Foster stands. "Thank you, Father George. Now, how about our festival in July?"

"I --have to be honest here: I don't want to leave until I've experienced just one St. Swithun's Day," I say carefully. "Perhaps I can come back for it."

"Leaving! Who's talking about *leaving*? We just got you fixed! Now that you're not broke any more, we can get to using you the way you're supposed to be used," booms Mr. Foster heartily.

"Don't you try to weasel out of this, Father George!" shouts Agnes Brown from the side of the room, in such a loud voice that she needs no mic. "We've had prayer groups going for you ever since you left, and in my new boyfriend's church, too. That sneaky Devil Drink had its wicked grips on you and wouldn't let go. My boyfriend has told me I have to forgive you, so that's what I'm doing, but I'll not be tempted any longer by your good looks or your smooth-talking ways! I've joined my boyfriend's Baptist church. Maybe God and these other people here can forgive you, but I'm not sure I can yet, so right after the ice cream parfait dessert here—this is my *boyfriend*, by the way—Harold, say hello. Wipe the crumbs off your mustache--!" (a short portly gentleman about Social Security age waves self-consciously from his seat)—"I'm saying good-by and turning in my choir robe."

There is a small chorus of "Amen!" Someone applauds and is promptly hushed.

"We're sure to miss you, Miss Brown. Thank you for your-- kind words and your service to the choir. But what about the Bishop? And your one dollar pledges? And the fact that you are a mission and a supply priest is taking care of you?" I am plainly baffled.

"Well. Fact is, Father George," says Mr. Campbell, "we all lied."

"And that's *another* reason I'm leaving!" yells Agnes Brown, standing up again. Her boyfriend struggles to rise. "Not before parfaits!" she tells him.

"What do you mean, you all lied?"

"We never changed our pledges, Father," says Mr. Foster. "We just said so, so's you could get some help."

"You—*lied* to the Bishop?"

"We don't look on it that way, Father," says a man at one of the side tables. "If he chose to think that we'd done that, we weren't about to correct him."

"Never correct a Bishop," agrees his wife. There is a round of head-bobbing.

"Excuse me," I murmur, and wipe my eyes with a napkin embroidered BBYC+ GC. There is so much honesty (even from Agnes Brown) and acceptance in this room that it takes all my fortitude not to break down and blubber like a baby.

"Now: Miss Peabody is going to play and sing a hymn." Miss Peabody moves to the piano. She is, I note, actually smiling! I realize we've never heard Miss

Peabody sing more than a measure of music, and that only during rehearsals.

She wields the mic again. "Before I sing I want to tell you all that this is my swan song."

There is a murmur of surprise.

"I took all the letters that I wrote from Edith Hatcher and I was gonna burn them, but my son Tom here persuaded me to publish them, so here they are!" She holds up a slick-covered book entitled "The Blue Church of Edith Hatcher".

"It's a murder mystery and my editor says it could turn into a best-seller! And I'm selling this first edition for ten dollars each! First hundred buyers get a book! See me after the brunch." She settles herself on the groaning piano bench and bursts into a chorus of "Jesus Loves Me, this I know/ For the Bible tells me so". The audience joins in, enthusiastically.

"Look at that woman," says Mother. "A weight's off her. You did it, George. I really wish now I'd heard you on the radio."

"I wish I'd heard me, too," I say.

"Listen, before we leave here I want to make sure you meet Ed."

"Ed? Who's Ed?"

"He's the man I told you about. We both play bridge. A widower. He goes to St. Barnabus'."

She points out a grey-haired man at a nearby table, who waves to us. He has a very nice smile, I note. "He gave me this orchid. Said it's not every day we celebrate the prodigal son's return."

I wave back. "Mother, I don't get it. Nobody's asked anything about Gail."

"Well, of course not. Those who know, understand. The rest never met her, so they wouldn't care one way or another."

I have to raise my voice to Miss Elliott to be heard: "Where's Mr. Leland Frye? Shouldn't he be playing? I don't see him here."

"Oh. After you left and he got married, he and --." I can't make out her next words,"—without saying anything."

"Ah." Well, I had warned the church, hadn't I? "Miss Elliott, who paid for all this today? All these people, even the children's—."

"I guess you'll find out sometime. We took the money out of the pipe organ gift donation."

"Ah-hah. Good idea." And it was. "I must have been flat-out drunk to think that a pipe organ would fit inside that size church."

"It's actually worse than that. Mrs. Gustafson was just leading you on when she told you she was giving a lot of money to the church and you thought it would be enough for a pipe organ. Truth is, it only paid for the two-manual Allen we bought. And this party."

"Huh. *So in the future I need to be cautious about trusting any old ladies who dance naked on the church lawn!*" I am aware suddenly from the laughter that Miss Peabody has stopped singing and I have shouted the last sentence.

"Sorry," I say, waving my hand, and people seem to think I have just given a blessing, because they're now getting up, chattering and moving chairs back from the tables. Miss Peabody rips into an oddly-chosen rendition of "The Beer Barrel Polka".

I lower my voice. "Wow. I sure got people's hopes up so for a pipe organ."

"I think you just wanted something wonderful for us, Father. And look at all of us here today! We've never been together like this, not even on St. Swithun's Day."

"Maybe we're starting a new tradition," I say. "Confession and then brunch."

"You look so different, Father George. I mean, it's not just your clothing—"

"I assure you that if I had known what was going to happen today I would have worn more formal clothes." Actually, until this moment I have not been sure I would ever put on my clerical robes again. Perhaps I have never been meant to be a priest. Perhaps some other career lies ahead of me.

Miss Elliott seems to read my thoughts. "Oh, Father, shame on you. You've been called to be a priest and you are one."

"How did you --?"

"How did your mother know when she named you? Could not God himself have broken in to whisper in her ear and claim you as His own? Miracles, Father. Look at me: I have a new grandmother!"

"Miss Elliott. Miss Elliott, I have two confessions to make. No, three."

"Oh. My."

"My first is an abject apology for your having had to see me, drunk and hung over, the morning that you came and gave me muffins."

"Father George," she says firmly, "when I was young I fell off my horse and broke my arm. And all the way to the hospital I kept trying to apologize to Dad, and he said, 'It's a broken arm. Could've happened to anyone. You're my same girl as you were before you fell. A broken arm doesn't make you less lovable.' Because that's how I felt—unlovable, not worthy of love. So *you* had a broken head. Just like I've got to be careful about putting too much pressure on this arm, you have to be careful not to put too much pressure on your head. Dad says you're still a lovable person. He says Betty knows good man-flesh when he's sitting on her back." And here she drops her gaze.

I stare at her, at a loss for words. "You said you had three confessions, Father. That's just one."

"Uh—oh, yes! The second is that not ever having been to brunch here, I exaggerated the menu in my mind and imagined the food would be quite exquisite and unusual."

"Like the Food of the Gods? Ambrosia on everything?"

"Something like that; but it really just tastes like the lunches I've had here, except for the champagne cocktails. Which you will note I have not touched."

"So you realize it isn't the food. It's the *company*, Father."

"My third confession is much harder. Much harder. Miss Elliott, I've-- never been able to remember your first name. And the time passed when I could have asked, but I was too embarrassed or ashamed, I don't know."

"I don't tell many people because I was bullied about it when I was young. You know I don't have a very loud voice except when I sing. Do you ever hear me over— the *rest* of the alto section?"

We both smile, since the "rest of the alto section" is-- *was* Agnes Brown.

"-- and in church when I was a child people would tease me and call me "Whispering Hope".

"Hope? *Hope is your name?*"

"Daddy named me. He said this way, no matter what happened, he'd always have Hope."

Now I crane my neck to look at her father and he actually winks at me.

I'm looking at two identical smiles of Hope.

*   *   *

I am vesting for the first time in months, sliding my white alb over my head in such a familiar long-unused way that I sigh with stagefright. There is a knock at the door to my little room which leads into the church, with a second door to the outside.

Is the service beginning already? I open the inside door.

Mr. Leland Frye stands there, a blue-wrapped package in his hands. His face is one of concern.

"What--? I thought you were gone!" I stammer.

"No, sir. Just that one Sunday. And then *you* left before I could explain myself. I waved to you from the church steps, but whoever was driving you didn't see me. I thought you waved to me, but when you didn't stop, I decided you must have been very angry with me for skipping out like that."

"I—what?"

"I apologized to the vestry and they explained what was happening. That supply priest we had knew *nothing* about music—not like you, Father George It was a real trial, playing for him! And then when I was giving Amber a lesson one afternoon and the whole organ just blew up—POP! just like that!--oh, I tell you, we were so scared!--, well, we had no choice but to go ahead and buy a new one. Again, I am so sorry that you weren't in on the decision—I know how very important that was to you."

"And is this a gift?"

"No. I—saved it from being put in with the auction items. It's your St. Swithun's book."

I tear open the blue paper, which falls to the floor. There in my hands is my journal, the lock dented, but unopened!

"Amber stole it. She was mad at you because Matthew had died, and she blamed you—who can tell, with kids?" Mr. Frye—(Lee)—sighs, stooping to pick up the blue paper. "Then her boyfriend tried to bust it open and she stopped him, but was afraid to give it back to you, so she gave it to me all wrapped, for the auction."

He pauses. "I'm afraid I peeked."

"You did!"

"I mean I peeked inside the wrapping, not the book itself. It must be a very valuable book. I don't think I ever saw you without it."

"Not so very valuable anymore. But I thank you, anyway. Thank you! Good to know that it's been in safe hands."

"I'm—I'm going to start the prelude now. Welcome back, Father George." We shuffle around the tiny room so he can get to the door. "Oh, I hope you don't mind—my husband Emilio is singing a solo to welcome you back."

For a moment a flash of anger washes over me— *What is happening to my beloved church? Is everything to be out of my control?* But then I stop myself and take a deep breath.

"I look forward to it," I say. Leland appears visibly relieved. "I'm going to play the gambe stop when he sings, just for you."

Alone, I sit in my little antechamber of a dressing room as the prelude begins. The music sounds enough like a pipe organ from here to mollify me. All the inner furor I felt about that damned gambe stop has left me. *Why was so I so intent on having it?* I wonder.

Another knock on my door, this time the crucifer. We step outside, past Mr. Campbell awaiting his signal to pull the church bell rope, and around to the front steps of the now-white church. Inside it is cool and it looks as though every seat has been taken. The ushers Tom Elliott and Mr. Foster, handing out programs, both nod to me. Even the choir pews are full. The sound of the organ music in Lee's expert hands surrounds the walls.

And, to be painfully honest, I cannot tell if the gambe stop is on or not.

And then like a message from Heaven I hear it: *Gail's voice!* I peer around. But it is that of a young black-haired man singing "Ave Maria" in Latin—the Schubert, not the Bach-Gounod, I am pleased to hear, (although a Roman Catholic sort of choice—I shall have to schedule a meeting with Mr. --with Lee-- for future edification) -- in such a pure falsetto (*Fortunate man. He could have been a eunuch in another era*), that I do nothing more than seize the moment and inwardly rejoice.

"This is the day, this is the day that the Lord has made!" sings the choir and their dozen voices harmonize with no droning undertone! The congregation joins in.

And what is that in their hands? Are those—*Praise books?*

The end

Made in the USA
Charleston, SC
28 July 2015